Airport Nurse

Rose Williams

THORNDIKE
CHIVERS

20174521

This Large Print edition is published by Thorndike Press®,
Waterville, Maine USA and by BBC Audiobooks Ltd,
Bath, England.

Published in 2006 in the U.S. by arrangement with Maureen
Moran Agency.

Published in 2006 in the U.K. by arrangement with the author.

U.S. Hardcover   0-7862-8790-X   (Candlelight)
U.K. Hardcover 10: 1 4056 3872 9   (Chivers Large Print)
U.K. Hardcover 13: 978 1 405 63872 2
U.K. Softcover   10: 1 4056 3873 7   (Camden Large Print)
U.K. Softcover   13: 978 1 405 63873 9

The text of this Large Print edition is unabridged.
Other aspects of the book may vary from the original edition.

Set in 16 pt. Plantin by Christina S. Huff.

Printed in the United States on permanent paper.

British Library Cataloguing-in-Publication Data available

Library of Congress Cataloging-in-Publication Data

Williams, Rose, 1912–
     Airport nurse / by Rose Williams.
          p. cm. — (Thorndike Press large print Candlelight)
     ISBN 0-7862-8790-X (lg. print : hc : alk. paper)
     1. Nurses — Fiction.   2. Airports — Fiction.
     3. Smuggling — Investigation — Fiction.   4. Large type
     books.   I. Title.   II. Series: Thorndike Press large print
     Candlelight series.
     PR9199.3.R5996A36 2006
     813′.54—dc22   2006010066

To my Aunt Tillie
— Mrs. Aubrey MacDonald.

Airport Nurse

Chapter One

Nurse Clare Andrews stood watching the giant Boeing 707-320 jet at its loading platform. From her vantage point on the glass-walled promenade of Trans-Continental Air Lines V.I.P. lounge, she had a perfect view of the runways. It was four-fifteen on a warm, sunny May afternoon, and the big gray jet with its red, white and blue circle trademark of the line was due to leave at four-thirty. Most of the passengers from the lounge reserved for important persons had already started down to board the flight, so her afternoon's work was almost over.

"Nurse!" A plaintive call from behind her caused Clare to wheel around quickly. She saw a gaudily dressed, middle-aged woman standing in the doorway of the lounge. Recognizing her at once as Stephanie Greenwald, the cosmetics queen, she quickly went over to her.

"Yes, Miss Greenwald," she said in the quiet, attentive manner which she maintained in dealing with the temperamental world of V.I.P.'s.

Stephanie Greenwald's heavy make-up did not conceal the fact that the over dressed woman was looking ill. "I'm not well at all," she complained. "I don't know whether I should board the plane or not."

Clare showed proper concern. "If you're really ill, perhaps you shouldn't."

The cosmetic queen's broad, ordinary face, which matched her squat figure, registered anger. "But I have to be in London for an important business conference to-morrow," she said.

"Is there anything I can do?" Clare asked.

The older woman gave her a venomous look. "I had a hard enough time finding you. The lounge was empty when I came in just now."

Clare nodded. "I'm sorry," she said. "All the other passengers had left. And I often come out here to see the plane on its way."

"You know I'm a diabetic!" Stephanie Greenwald said.

"You have insulin with you," Clare suggested. "In case of airsickness, it's well to have a supply."

"I believe I have some tablets along," Stephanie Greenwald said, frowning. "It oughtn't to make any difference. If I should need attention, the stewardess could always give me an injection."

"Don't count on that," Clare warned her. "Stewardesses are not permitted to administer hypodermic injections to anyone."

The woman in the turban hat and boldly patterned black and white checked suit of mini-skirt length, quite unbecoming to her stocky figure, regarded her with an ominous glare. "I'm certain I had insulin from the stewardess when I crossed on Pan-American," she insisted.

"The rules are the same on every line," Clare assured her. "It is possible she may have had a supply of tablets. Or even orange juice, a candy bar or plain sugar can be used to give temporary relief."

Stephanie Greenwald was now digging into a large handbag. After a moment she lifted out a small plastic container with tablets. "I have them," she said, triumphantly showing them to Clare. Replacing them in her bag, she closed it and asked, "Could I have a glass of cold water?"

"Of course," Clare said, and rushed to get it. She'd been warned about the temperamental cosmetics queen when given a list of the flight's passengers. The demanding Stephanie had been a customer of most of the major air lines and never voiced satisfaction with any of them.

"We're her present target," the young man from the passenger department had told Clare wryly as he gave her the list of those to be expected in the V.I.P. lounge.

The stout woman was seated when Clare returned with the water. She took it and drank half the contents of the glass. "I feel better now," she said, returning it to Clare.

Clare glanced at her watch. "Perhaps you should start down," she said. "Your flight leaves in eight minutes."

Stephanie Greenwald looked disgruntled. "I hate flying," she said. "I have a nervous spell every time I board a plane."

Clare smiled in sympathy. "Many people feel the same way. But you'll forget all about it once you're on board. The weather predictions are good. You should have an easy flight. And this is a reasonably quiet craft."

"It better be!" was Stephanie Greenwald's grim comment as she got to her feet again. "I'm in a position to give this air line a large amount of business if they offer proper service. And if they do, they'll be the first!"

"Perhaps I'd better see you to the plane," Clare said, anxious to send the fussy woman on her way.

"It might be a wise idea," Stephanie Greenwald said at once.

Clare led her out to the down escalator and along the busy concourse to the ticket gate. They paused only briefly there, and then she escorted the touchy cosmetics queen across to the waiting jet, where one of the stewardesses took over.

Clare turned away from the boarding ramp with a sigh of relief. The jet was scheduled to leave in three or four minutes, and the disturbed Stephanie seemed to have no idea of time. As Clare passed the halfway mark on her way back to the terminal building, she saw a familiar figure coming toward her with a smile. It was Boyle Heath, the television star, and the only remaining name to be checked off her list.

He was hatless, and his dark hair was ruffled by the slight breeze. His tall, lean figure and handsome classic-features were familiar to her. Boyle Heath commuted to London regularly, since his hour mystery series was taped over there. Not only did she enjoy him as a debonair detective on television; he had also become a personal friend. She'd met him shortly after she'd been assigned to the V.I.P. lounge eighteen months before. Since then they'd dated quite a few times.

He was wearing one of his gray tweed suits with distinctive British styling and looking every inch a figure in some romantic spy story, even to the brief case he carried in his left hand. Pausing, he smiled at her and said, "Almost didn't get here! My cab was caught in a bad traffic jam in town."

"You had me worried," she said, returning his smile. "How long will you be away this time?"

"Depends," he told her. "We've got a half-dozen episodes of the show to do. I should be back for the weekend."

"Not if you don't hurry. You'll miss your flight."

He laughed. "Always on the job! That's you. I'll call you when I get back to New York."

"Do," she said, watching after him as he moved on quickly.

By the time she reached the terminal, the boarding ramp had been pulled back from the massive shining jet. Fuel truck, mail truck, jeeps and luggage carriers moved a distance away. Then the big jet edged forward. Not needing any time to warm up, it proceeded slowly away from the taxiway to the runway and turned its nose to the far end. Then, with a tremendous roar, it began its run. Picking up speed incredibly fast, it forged straight ahead and thrust itself into the air, climbing some two thousand feet a minute. Before she could count ten, it was out of sight.

Its going marked the end of her working day. With a small sigh of relief, she went back inside the large Trans-Continental Building. Large or small, she always found an airport a stimulating place: the waiting rooms with their many ticket counters, the flight boards with their lists of faraway cities, the announcements coming over the loudspeakers in several languages and the piles of luggage with hotel and air line stickers from all over the world. The people were interesting as well, especially at Kennedy Airport, where one regularly saw ladies in saris and men wearing every type of hat from a ten-gallon Stetson to a turban.

Making her way to the dressing room where she'd change from her neat blue uniform and cap to street clothes, she briefly reviewed her experiences since she had come to New York from her training in a small hospital in Nebraska. At first she'd worked in one of the big public hospitals in the city. Then, on a trip home, the stewardess on her plane had asked her, "Have you ever thought of working for an air line?"

"No," Clare had said. "I don't think I like flying well enough to want to do it every day."

"There are plenty of ground jobs," the stewardess had assured her.

Clare looked up at the girl in surprise. "Really? For a nurse?"

"Quite a few," the girl said. "There are nurses on duty at all the big terminals. The hours are good and the work is interesting. You should investigate it."

Clare promised that she would as soon as she returned to New York. The idea appealed to her. Being brought up in a small town had made her hungry to enjoy some of the glamor of big city life. And she wasn't finding much of it in the public hospital ward where her duties kept her. Not that she wasn't a dedicated nurse; she enjoyed helping the sick. But it seemed reasonable to try for a change of background. There were plenty of desperately ill people who had to use the air lines. She could still do important work and get to know another side of nursing.

When she was home, she discussed it with her mother. Clare was one of four children, and her widowed mother had kept the family together on the small pension left when Clare's father was killed in an industrial accident, plus what she earned as a practical nurse. It had been her mother's nursing that had interested Clare in becoming a trained nurse. Her sister was married, with two youngsters of her own, and her two brothers, both younger, were still in high school.

Clare's mother was a buxom, good-natured woman. She'd listened to her daughter with interest. "I think you should consider an air line job," she said finally. "It would give you a better chance to meet nice young men."

Clare blushed. "That's not why I'm thinking of changing my work," she protested.

"Still, it is a matter to be considered," her mother said in her frank way. "I'd like to see you married with a good home."

"I have lots of time for that!"

"Maybe not as much as you think!" was her mother's comment.

Clare was somewhat shaken by the firm note in her mother's voice. Later, when she was in her own room, the memory of what had been said made her stare into the mirror and consider herself. At twenty-three, she certainly didn't look like an old maid! Her short-cropped blonde hair in the Twiggy style topped an oval face with pleasant, even features, if you disregarded the fact that her nose was a trifle snubbed. Her blue eyes were large and nicely spaced, and her ready smile showed gleaming white teeth.

When she returned to New York, she began a round of the air line companies. Her most interesting job offer came from the Trans-Continental line. The sober young executive who had interviewed her had offered her the job in the V.I.P. lounge, and she'd been quick to accept it. Not only had it led to her meeting dozens of celebrities; it had also given her a pleasant atmosphere in which to carry on her nursing. There had been a number of emergencies during her more than a year on duty, but she had come to feel at home in the responsible position

She had also taken an apartment not far from Kennedy Airport with another girl who worked in the finance department of the airline. She was from Ohio, a redhead named Hester Carson. Clare found her easygoing and ideal to share living quarters with. Hester was engaged to a pilot with the line, and when Clare went out with Harry Travis they often made it a double date.

Harry Travis was someone who had come to play an important role in Clare's busy life. She had met him the second day she was on duty in the V.I.P. lounge. He'd approached

16

her in the company of a bearded, brown-skinned man in a turban and a gray silk business suit.

Harry had introduced himself as a junior executive in the main office of Trans-Continental and then had her meet his companion in the turban. He was the Indian representative of Trans-Continental, on his way home.

"Mr. Rajput has something in his eye," Harry had told her. "He's not looking forward to a long journey by plane with it bothering him."

Clare nodded. "Is his flight soon due?"

"Not for an hour," Harry had said. The brown-skinned man had offered a sad little smile and nodded to indicate this was so.

"If you'll come into my office," Clare told the man from India, "I'll see what I can do. You may have to see a doctor."

She spent a quarter-hour examining the eye and then washing it out with boric acid. This didn't seem to help, so she tried several drops of mineral oil in an effort to flush away the source of irritation. After a few moments the brown-skinned man began to smile and told her his eye was better.

Harry Travis had thanked her and then had taken the man from India to his plane.

17

Clare soon forgot Mr. Rajput, but she kept thinking of Harry Travis. He was a brisk, sharp-eyed young man, with crew-cut brown hair and a pleasant face.

Several days later he returned to the V.I.P. lounge to see her again. He wasted no time getting down to the reason for his visit. He wanted to take her to dinner. She saw no reason to refuse. And that was how their friendship had begun. It was taken for granted by those who knew them they would soon announce their engagement, but Clare didn't think their relationship was that serious. Otherwise she wouldn't have started going out occasionally with the television star, Boyle Heath. Her friend Hester accused her of doing it to make Harry jealous, but that wasn't true.

As she made her way down to the busy waiting room she was met by a pale young man who worked in the main office. She remembered little about him except that his name was Roberts.

Roberts offered her a nervous smile. "I missed you at the lounge and was just going to the dressing room to find you. Mr. Benson wants to see you in his office."

Clare showed surprise. Arnold Benson was the head of Trans-Continental's main office. She said, "The big boss himself!"

"That's right, Miss Andrews," Roberts said in his mild way. "He'd like to see you at once."

"Thanks," Clare said. Roberts nodded and walked on. She headed toward the escalator leading to the second floor where the executive offices were located, wondering what she'd done wrong. She surely must have made some major blunder to be called before the manager in this fashion. She'd met him only once before, and he'd struck her as an aloof, cold man. He was tall, bald and wore rimless glasses. In her brief meeting with him on that previous occasion, he'd spoken to her crisply, and his steely gray eyes had never ceased appraising her. Arnold Benson had the reputation of being ruthless where the welfare of the air line was concerned. She made her way to the desk of his receptionist, certain she was in trouble.

Chapter Two

The prim secretary outside Arnold Benson's private office looked up at her and said, "Are you Miss Andrews?"

"Yes," Clare said, feeling momentarily even more unsure of herself.

"Mr. Benson will see you right away," the prim one said. She rose, went to the door and tapped on it gently. Then she opened it and announced Clare.

Clare entered the large white-walled office with its heavy crimson carpet, broad desk and easy chairs in the same shade as the carpet. The walls were decorated with photographs of various aircraft famous in the company's history. Arnold Benson, smiling icily, came around the desk to greet her.

"Thank you for coming so promptly," he said. "Won't you please sit down?" As she did so, he went on, "I suppose you have been wondering why I sent for you."

"Yes, I have," Clare admitted.

The tall bald man stood before her, his

appraising, gray eyes studying her from behind rimless glasses. "You've been with us quite a while now, Miss Andrews."

"Almost two years," she said.

He nodded. Placing his hands behind his back, he rocked very slightly on his heels. "We've been very pleased with your work."

Her smile was incredulous. "There have been no complaints?"

"None," he said. "That's not why you're here. I've brought you here to ask a favor. May I depend on your discretion?"

"Of course," she said.

"Our company finds itself involved in a most unpleasant business," Arnold Benson went on in his rasping voice. "And I'm going to ask you to help us clear our name."

Clare was becoming increasingly confused. She failed to see where she fitted into the situation the general manager of Trans-Continental was describing. But, she said, "I'll do anything I can."

"Excellent attitude," the thin, bald man said approvingly. "I'm going to give you all the facts. In confidence, of course. You are not to reveal what I'm about to tell you to anyone."

"I understand," she said.

"For some time quantities of valuable diamonds have been smuggled into this country through the Port of New York," he said, "some of them from dealers in Europe and others representing thefts on the other side. The authorities here have been gradually eliminating suspects. They've even caught some of the fences who've handled the smuggled and stolen jewels and a few other minor figures in the smuggling ring. They've learned enough to know that shipments have been arriving on our overseas flights."

"How could they know?" she asked.

"Because of the time the shipments reached New York," Arnold Benson said. "Because they picked up several of the underlings here at our terminal waiting for the London noon flight to come in."

"How do you think I can help?"

"In a very general way," the bald man said, the hard gray eyes fixed on her. "The Federal men think whoever is the principal agent uses our London service frequently. They also believe the man or woman who is bringing the stuff over is probably one of those who has access to the V.I.P. lounge. They suspect it may be a well-known figure using his prominence to help him in the commission of their crime."

She frowned. "But isn't this a matter for trained experts? For the customs?"

"The customs men assigned to our terminal have been giving all overseas passengers and their baggage special surveillance, and it hasn't helped," Arnold Benson declared. "Last week another lot of stolen jewels was smuggled through. We have been asked to cooperate in halting this criminal activity."

"I'll be glad to do anything I can," Clare said. "But I don't see how I can be of any help."

"Don't worry about it," he said harshly, moving around to seat himself behind the broad desk. "You are not the only one I'm enlisting to help in this. A number of our people will be keeping on the alert for any suspicious act on the part of one of our passengers. If enough eyes are watching, the guilty person is bound to make some slip which will be noticed. The Federal men already suspect three persons who make an unusually large number of round trips overseas on our jets."

"And you want me to keep a close eye on them?"

"Exactly," Arnold Benson said as he opened a desk drawer on the right and drew out a neat folder. From it he carefully took a single typed sheet of paper. Raising his eyes to give Clare a piercing glance, he then turned his attention to the paper and read, "Gloria Faith, motion picture actress." He also gave her Park Avenue address and the number of times she'd journeyed to London and back in the previous twelve months. It came to the astonishing total of sixteen times.

"Miss Faith has been giving concerts in England," Clare explained. "Since she's given up making films, she's been doing a lot of singing."

"Isn't it rather that films gave her up?" the bald man inquired icily. "Let us speak plainly, Miss Andrews. You must be well aware that Gloria Faith is a chronic alcoholic who has been slipping badly in the entertainment world."

"She has been drinking heavily," Clare agreed. "The last time she was in the lounge she was in very bad shape. I worried about her boarding the plane."

Arnold Benson nodded. "I've been informed she's going steadily deeper in debt, in spite of pushing herself to do these so-called concerts when she's often in no fit condition to appear before the public. The Federal men think that in her desperation she may very well have thrown in her lot with these jewel thieves."

"I can't believe it!" Clare protested.

"She's always been so nice to me. Have they thoroughly searched her each trip?"

"They have, and without any success," Arnold Benson went on in his harsh tone. "As you perhaps know, Miss Faith is in Europe at this moment." He paused. "Now I'll proceed to the next name: Fritz Manner."

Again Clare was surprised. Fritz Manner was a suave, gray-haired man with a slight accent who had the reputation of being an international financier. He dressed extremely well and always had a swarthy man in attendance on him to whom he'd referred as his secretary when chatting with Clare in the lounge one day. He was very friendly and easy to please, and she had imagined he was extremely rich.

"Would Fritz Manner be interested in anything like that?" she ventured. "I mean, he's so wealthy anyway."

The bald man shook his head and smiled grimly. "You are wrong in that. Manner is treading on extremely thin ice. He has over extended himself both in Europe and here. He, too, is badly in need of ready money; desperate enough to make him also a suspect."

"I'm sorry," she said. "He's always been so considerate."

"I appreciate that you may have found

him pleasant," the general manager of the air line said stiffly. "But that does not exclude him from this list. And now we come to the third name. René Le Blanc."

Clare at once pictured the willowy Frenchman, with his exquisite manners and fine features; a familiar figure in the V.I.P. lounge in beret, turtleneck sweater and elegantly tailored sports clothes. He was world famous as an amateur racing car driver and had recently been divorced from his jetset American wife.

She said, "He and Claudia Craig have just been divorced."

The bald man nodded. "She finally got rid of him. And he didn't get a penny in settlement. So he's really in a bad way for money." The manager paused. "In fact, I suspect him beyond the others. I believe he is our man. The question is: How does he get the jewels through customs?"

"He doesn't have to be the guilty one," she pointed out. "Even the Federal men must have doubts, since they named the other two."

"Admittedly," the general manager agreed with icy reluctance. "But I still cling to my own theory. All three of these people will be passing through the V.I.P. lounge in the next week or ten days. And I'd appreciate it if you'd watch them as closely as you can and report directly to me anything that raises your suspicions."

"I'll do my best," she said. "We handle quite a lot of people. And often my attention if fully taken by someone who is ill."

"I understand that," he said. "I don't want you to interfere with your nursing duties. But I would appreciate any help you can offer." He paused significantly. "It may be that none of these people is guilty. The Federal men also have their eye on our own staff. At the moment they are in doubt about one of our overseas pilots, a stewardess and a man with executive standing in the company. So it may turn out that a member of the Trans-Continental family is to blame."

"It should certainly make everyone feel better to have it cleared up," she said, thinking of the dark shadow that now hung over so many.

"That goes without saying," Arnold Benson said, standing up. "Thank you for bearing with me, Miss Andrews. Please be on the alert. I'll call you in again if I receive any further information."

Clare rose, knowing this was her dismissal. After a few words in parting, she awkwardly made her way out. The loud an-

27

nouncement of a flight leaving for San Francisco filled her ears as she turned and crossed the waiting room to the exit.

She had a date with Harry Travis. The young executive had tickets for the new play at the Vivian Beaumont Theatre at Lincoln Center. He came by for Clare in his car, and they drove into the city. She had been looking forward to the performance, which was a revival of Sheridan's "The Rivals," but now the evening seemed ruined for her. The revelations made her by the company's general manager had left her on edge. And he had pledged her to secrecy, which meant she couldn't say anything to Harry.

He noticed her silence and general uneasiness during the drive. Giving her a sharp side-glance, he asked, "Aren't you feeling well?"

She attempted a smile. "I guess I'm tired."

"I thought it might be because Boyle Heath left for London today," he said with irony.

"Harry, please! Don't start on that tonight," she pleaded, glancing out at the passing traffic on the busy expressway.

"Sorry," he said.

"You'd better be," she reprimanded him, her eyes still away from him.

By the time they'd left the car in a parking

lot and leisurely walked across the wide expanse of asphalt leading to the theatre, she felt better. They stood for a moment beside the great pool directly before its entrance and enjoyed the warm spring evening. Then they went inside and took their seats for the performance.

The large theatre was filled to capacity, and the company was excellent. For a time Clare forgot everything else in her enjoyment of the play. During the intermission they made plans to visit a favorite restaurant in the area which they hoped wouldn't be too crowded after the show.

It wasn't until they reached the tiny rendezvous with its red tablecloths and flickering candles set in the necks of wax-coated wine bottles that they began to talk freely. When they finished their discussion of the play, they turned to happenings at work. And Clare received her first surprise.

Giving her an earnest glance across the table, Harry said, "You probably don't know it, but we've got a smuggling ring using our overseas flights."

She stared at him. "How do you know?"

"Part of my job," he assured her. "I can't go into the details, but from what I've heard they're casting a sharp eye on a lot of people."

Clare was relieved to have this chance to bring the subject out into the open. At least it relieved her tensions. However, she had an idea that Harry didn't guess she'd been fully briefed on the problem by none other than Arnold Benson himself. And because the general manager had pledged her to secrecy, she made up her mind to pretend innocence in the matter.

"What sort of smuggling?"

"Stolen jewelry," he said. "Mostly diamonds. It's a big money racket. I hear they're watching one of the pilots."

"Any idea who?" she asked.

He shook his head. "No. They're being pretty close-mouthed."

"Dick is a pilot on the overseas run," she reminded him. Dick was the young man Hester expected to marry.

Harry's pleasant face registered doubt. "It wouldn't be Dick."

"How can you be sure?"

He frowned. "We both know Dick. He's a wonderful fellow. He's engaged to Hester."

Clare said, "He could still be guilty. He is one of the pilots flying directly into London."

"There are a good many. Why pick on Dick? You want to get Hester upset?" he asked indignantly.

"I just want to be sure she's protected," Clare said firmly. "In a thing like this, you never can tell who the guilty person might be."

"I'd be willing to guarantee it isn't Dick," the young man said just as staunchly.

Remembering that Arnold Benson had also mentioned a stewardess and one of the executive staff as possible suspects, she went on to question him. "Is it only this pilot they suspect?"

"No. There are others. But I haven't heard who they are." He gave her a warning look. "You better not say anything about what I've told you to Hester or anyone else."

She pretended surprise. "Is it all that secret?"

"We're not supposed to talk about it. The boss is hot to get the thing nipped," Harry told her. "It will be a major scandal if any of the newspapers get hold of the story."

"And Trans-Continental is a very conservative company," she said with a faint smile.

"Arnold Benson hates any kind of bad publicity," Harry agreed. "I wouldn't want the newspapers to quote me on the story. So just keep what I've told you to yourself."

"I won't say a word," she promised.

"I'll be going over to the London office next week," he said. "I may get some more information there. After all, it concerns them as much as it does us."

She smiled. "You'll be leaving just about the time Boyle Heath comes back."

"Great for you," Harry said with a wry smile. "Makes it easy for you to juggle your dates between us."

"I didn't say that," she protested.

"I know what you were thinking," the crew-cut young man said.

He saw her back to the apartment but didn't go in, because it was late and Hester was already in bed and asleep. Standing at the door with her, he said, "Remember, don't mention anything about the smuggling business to Hester."

She smiled. "Yes, sir."

"I'm serious," he said. And he took her in his arms for a good night kiss. He let her go with a mocking smile. "Bet pal Boyle couldn't match that!"

He was on his way to the stairs before she could offer him a reprimand. With a despairing little smile, she turned and let herself into the apartment. Only the night light was on, and she made her way across to her own room, not wanting to wake Hester. It had been a strange evening, full of tension and surprises.

When she awoke, the odor of bacon and

eggs was in the air, and she heard Hester busily engaged in the kitchen. She hastily threw back the bed-clothes and groped for her slippers.

It took her only a few minutes to wash and dress. Hester was already seated at the blue arborite kitchen table when Clare joined her. The pretty redhead gave her a smiling greeting.

"You were late getting in. I had an idea you wouldn't feel like making breakfast."

"And it was my turn," Clare said contritely. "I'll do it for the next two days." She gulped down her orange juice and then spread some marmalade on a thin slice of unbuttered toast.

"Don't worry about it," Hester said. "I like preparing breakfast. I always used to do it at home. How was the play?"

"Good," Clare said as she poured herself a cup of black coffee. "We went to a restaurant afterward."

"Lucky you!" the redhead said. "The theatre and a restaurant afterward, while I sat here all evening alone. That's what I rate for falling in love with a pilot who is always off in some other part of the world!"

Clare smiled over her coffee. "Harry is going to London next week."

"And Boyle Heath will be back in New

York to squire you again," Hester told her. "You just can't lose!"

There was some more banter between them before they hurried down to catch the bus that delivered them at the airport. Clare had barely time to change into her uniform and get to her post in the V.I.P. lounge before a number of passengers for early flights began to arrive. She compared notes with the stewardess assigned to duty with her in the lounge and saw that all the arrivals who wanted coffee were served it.

About two dozen people were gathered waiting for flights to the West Coast and the South. It was another pleasant day, and sun beamed in through the glass walls of the luxuriously furnished lounge. Clare moved around quietly, chatting with some of the important ones who seemed most impatient. The music from the Muzak system was playing softly, and she noted by the large clock on the center pillar that the first flight would be departing in about fifteen minutes.

The atmosphere of peace and quiet was suddenly broken by a loud scream from the other end of the big room. A woman shouted, "That man has collapsed!"

Clare lost no time hurrying to the side of the fallen man. He was one of the Southbound passengers taking the Dallas flight. She'd noticed him because of the big Stetson that he wore. He was a rangy youth with a tanned outdoor look, marred only by dark-rimmed glasses. Now he was stretched out on the carpet, his hat fallen to one side. She knelt by him and saw that he was suffering from some sort of seizure. His eyes were closed, but his mouth twitched and his hands opened and closed in a repetitive fashion. It took her only a moment to judge the symptoms and decide he was an epileptic suffering from a psychomotor attack.

Glancing up, she told the circle of onlookers, "He'll be all right. Please move away. Don't crowd him!"

At the same time she quickly administered to the stricken young man. After loosening his tie and collar, she turned him on his side. It was only a matter of a minute before the attack was over and he stared up at her with dazed eyes.

"Where am I," he asked.

"At the airport," she said. "Don't you remember?"

He raised himself a little, looking pale and shaken. "I guess so," he mumbled, shamefaced and awkward. "When I'm sick like this it takes me a few minutes to get things straight."

"You have plenty of time," she assured him, still on her knees at his side. "Your flight is the second one. You still have nearly a half-hour."

"I was going home," he said weakly, looking at her with a questioning expression.

"That's right," she agreed. "Do you think you need a doctor?"

The Texan showed alarm. "No. I'll be all right now. I've got pills with me. I'll take one." He got to his feet and straightened his glasses. Giving a self-conscious glance around him, he said, "I sure made a fool of myself."

"It doesn't matter," she said. "I'll get you some water, and you'd better take that pill right away."

Returning with the water, she waited until he took the pill. He gave her an unhappy glance. "I could feel it coming on, but I couldn't help myself."

"I know," she said. "You should always take care of yourself if there is time. Lie down and loosen your collar. Let anyone nearby know what is wrong. Have you had this condition long?"

"Long enough," the young man said grimly. He returned the empty glass to her. "I'm much obliged," he said. "My head is good and clear again."

"If you're feeling better, I think you should board your plane right away," she suggested.

The Texan was anxious to cooperate. "Whatever you say, miss."

"I'll go down with you," she said casually, not wanting to alarm him or have him protest her action. Fortunately, he was in a submissive mood and said nothing as they made their way to the escalator and the concourse. She saw him through the ticket gate and over to the boarding ramp, where she waited until he was on the plane. Afterward she confided to the stewardess with the passenger list that he'd just had an epileptic seizure and asked that she keep a special watch on him.

This done, she hurried back to the V.I.P. lounge. There was an overseas flight coming up, and a few of the passengers were beginning to arrive for it. She'd just received the sheet with the names of those scheduled for the flight and was standing checking it in when a man came up to her.

Lifting her eyes, she saw it was none other than the international playboy, René Le Blanc. The handsome young Frenchman wore his usual dark blue beret, a brown sport coat, fawn trousers and a white turtleneck sweater. He smiled at her.

"Are you not pleased to see me again?" he wanted to know.

Recalling the discussion with Arnold Benson the previous night, she had a hard time concealing her uneasiness.

She said, "I'm surprised. It seems to me you've just gotten back from a trip to Europe. I hadn't come on your name in my list yet."

He laughed lightly. "You will find me there, Miss Andrews. You see, I have not forgotten your name."

"I'm flattered," she said.

"You needn't be," he assured her with his usual charm. "You are an extremely pretty girl in America, the land of pretty girls."

She smiled. "What takes you overseas today?"

He gave her a mocking look. "A friend is having a birthday celebration. It would cause great unhappiness if I did not appear."

"Wonderful!" she said. "I wish I had your attitude toward time and money."

"Neither have too much importance for me," René Le Blanc said. "Perhaps you'll let me explain my philosophy to you when I come back."

She regarded him with her head slightly to one side. "Maybe," she said. "I'm a busy girl most of the time."

"But not while you are off duty," he protested with Gallic charm. "I shall wait until
you leave, and we'll find a romantic spot
somewhere. I have an idea you might be a
great help to me."

The words could be innocent enough, but
knowing what she did, Clare doubted it. She
suddenly had an idea the worldly René was
working out some scheme to make her an
accomplice in his smuggling game.

Chapter Three

Clare summoned a smile for the famed playboy. "You make it sound very interesting," she said.

"I promise it will be," he said, glancing around with an air of disapproval at the others gathered in the lounge. "You shouldn't be here at the beck and call of these fat rich old cows and their husbands. A girl with your ability is silly to go on working at a menial task."

"I've never considered nursing menial," she was quick to tell him.

"But no!" he agreed, a perplexed look on his handsome face. "I do not always express myself so well. To be a nurse is a dedication. But surely what you are doing here is not nursing in the best sense."

It was her turn to be on the defensive. "I feel I'm doing a useful job."

"That is true," he said. "But only a job. I can offer you a career a good deal more glamorous, and one that will pay many times what you can earn here."

She said, "Thanks. If you'll excuse me, there are some other people I have to check with before take-off time."

"Of course," he said politely. "But remember — I shall expect to see you when I return. We must have our talk."

"Enjoy your trip," she said, dismissing him with a polite smile as she moved on to interview one of the elderly matrons concerning whom he'd made disparaging comments.

While she carried on a routine conversation with one part of her mind, the other was occupied with what René Le Blanc had said to her. Today had been the first time he'd really shown her much attention. Previously he'd merely smiled and passed the time of day. Of course his wife had nearly always been with him during those other meetings, which would make a difference.

But there had been an urgency in his approach to her just now that made her wonder if he was the smuggler the Federal men were looking for.

The stout, well-dressed woman to whom she'd been casually speaking while these thoughts were running through her mind said rather sharply, "You haven't answered my question!"

"I'm sorry," Clare replied, flustered and

turning her mind to coping with the moment. "I missed what you said."

"I've asked you twice," the woman told her with a frown. "I wanted to know if the air line had special arrangements with any of the hotels. I know the Hilton chain has a special deal with one of the major air lines to give their passengers preferred bookings."

"We don't have," Clare said at once. "But we do make reservations with a number of good hotels. If you like, I'll take your name and look after it for you."

"No need," the woman said haughtily. "I already have my booking at the Westbury. I was just curious as to how you managed these things. It would seem you don't give them much special attention."

Clare was in no mood to argue the point. And she was relieved when the sound system interrupted with an announcement to the effect that London-bound passengers should make their way to the ticket gate. She smiled at the woman and took a stand by the double glass doors as the people began to file out. Jaunty René Le Blanc was almost the last to go. He paused to smile and wink at her.

"You will not forget?" he asked.

She smiled faintly. "I will depend on your memory."

"Next week, then," he said, "when I return." And he moved out.

She offered a smiling nod to the last of the passengers, an elderly man with a bleak expression and a cigar clamped in his mouth. Then the big lounge was empty again except for herself and Isobel, the stewardess on duty with her.

Clare walked out to the promenade and watched as the passengers who had recently left the lounge filed out onto the asphalt runway and crossed to the boarding ramp. The majority of them would be traveling first class, although occasionally someone would prefer the regular section.

The sun glistened on the big Boeing jet, bringing out the solid beauty of its clean lines. Within a few minutes it would be rising from the runway to nose out over the Atlantic. Its full load of pampered passengers would recline in ease for some hours until the plane touched down again at London airport. Then watches would be set ahead, and they'd quickly fit into the pattern of that other world.

Isobel, a tall blonde girl with an attractive smile, came out to join Clare. "I never get over the excitement," she said. "Every time a big plane leaves, I go with it in imagination."

Clare glanced at her in surprise. "You spent quite a while on the trans-Atlantic run. I should think you'd be bored by it all."

"Not a bit," Isobel said, her eyes fixed on the jet. "See the mechanics! They've just finished a last moment inspection. If they found a single bolt not as it should be, the flight would be held up. The fuel trucks have moved back, so they'll soon be ready to leave. Ad now the boarding ramp is being taken away. In a moment the girls will be standing in their sections explaining the use of life belts and emergency exists. Then the routine of serving meals and drinks will begin."

Clare smiled. "You sound nostalgic."

Isobel nodded. "I am. I wouldn't mind being in London tonight. It's lovely at this time of year."

"What made you transfer to duty here if you prefer flying?" Clare asked in mild surprise.

Isobel sighed. "It was that or give up stewardess work completely."

"Oh?"

The blonde girl in her trim uniform and cap nodded. "My mother had a serious operation. She hasn't made a good recovery. She needs me at home. There's no one else.

I have a woman who comes in during the day while I'm here."

"I'm sorry," Clare said with sincerity. "I didn't know. I hope she'll get better."

Isobel kept staring at the jet as it began slowly to head toward the runway. But the look of excitement had been replaced by a clouded expression. "I'm afraid that's too much to expect," she said.

Clare felt sorry for the tall girl and realized how little she'd known about her or her problems. It was amazing that you could work side by side with a person and yet remain a comparative stranger.

"We'll have a little breathing time before the arrivals begin for the Chicago special," Clare said.

"Not too long," the other girl warned her. She turned to give Clare her full attention now that the jet was out of sight. "I saw that the jet set's favorite playboy was giving you plenty of attention."

Clare laughed. "You mean René Le Blanc?"

"Who else?"

"He was just filling in time," Clare said.

"Don't be too certain," Isobel told her. "Now that he's divorced, he's probably looking for a new wife. He has an addiction to marrying."

"Marrying wealthy women," Clare reminded her. "And I'm certainly not a likely prospect."

"Who knows?" Isobel said. "He may have finally decided to try marrying for simple old love. Don't lose hope!"

The morning passed quickly, and soon it was lunch time. Things had slowed down again in the V.I.P. lounge, so Clare left Isobel to deal with any strays who wandered in between flights and went down to the employees' cafeteria for her noon snack. She rarely had more than a salad and a glass of milk, but the break was welcome.

The employees' cafeteria had an institutional look. Unlike the areas of Trans-Continental's Kennedy Airport Terminal that catered to passengers, it was drably decorated. In fact, it was bare of any of the ornate touches that made the main part of the terminal a show place. But to do the company justice, the service was fast and the food good.

Clare often shared a table with some other employee of the line, frequently with Harry. Now he came in a moment after her, and they took their places in line to make their choices.

After they had filled their trays, they found an unoccupied table and sat down.

Harry, who had helped himself to a hearty serving of roast beef with whipped potatoes, coffee and custard pie eyed her salad and milk with amusement.

"Still watching the calories," he teased her.

She made a pert face at him. "I have to stay thin and beautiful if I'm going to land a handsome husband."

"Just as long as I know your intentions," he said. "I was hoping you preferred fat men."

"Because you're planning to be one doesn't mean they're glamorous," she said, beginning to eat her salad.

"What's new in the V.I.P. department?" Harry wanted to know.

She smiled. "René Le Blanc flew to London this morning. He gave me quite a line."

"He should be an expert," was Harry's comment as he busied himself with his roast beef.

"Anything new about the smuggling?" she asked.

He gave her a warning look. "That's better not mentioned here."

"Oh?"

"You never know who's listening," Harry said, glancing around nervously. Then he told her, "I said it was very hot. Not everyone is supposed to know."

"I'm sorry," she said.

"There's nothing new, if you must have an answer," he went on. "The big story today is that the company is ordering a whole new fleet of jets for domestic flights."

Clare had heard rumors that this might happen. "I was told they had it in mind," she said. "Won't that mean faster service?"

"Faster and safer," he agreed. "But it's going to cost plenty. And we haven't paid for the jets in overseas service yet."

She smiled at him over her salad. "All you people in the business office do is worry about what operations department spends."

Harry showed great seriousness. "Someone has to worry. If we didn't put a brake on spending, we'd be bankrupt in no time. We've expanded fast. We didn't have a single overseas flight twenty years ago. In fact, hardly any of the companies did. And now the air lanes over the Atlantic are crowded day and night."

"Orville Wright and his brother didn't know what they were starting!"

"It's no joking matter," he said. "I'm all for buying this new lot of jets, but you sometimes wonder where all the money is going to come from."

"From more passengers?"

He nodded. "Traffic is bound to be heavier, with ocean liners gradually going out of favor. And increased speed will make air travel more appealing. In a few years we'll have supersonic jets crossing the Atlantic in an hour and a half."

"The V.I.P.'s will like that," she said. "They're always so impatient."

"I don't know how you stand catering to them," Harry said. "You're welcome to that pampered lot."

"You're jealous because I meet all the 'in' crowd," she teased him.

"Wet nurse to wastrels!" he said scornfully.

Their lunch together ended on this familiar note.

The afternoon in the V.I.P. lounge began like many other afternoons. A grim-faced captain of finance who was taking a flight to Hawaii harangued Clare about having had a nearly fatal attack of hypoxia on a previous flight.

"I have a cardiac ailment, you know," the hawk-faced man told her.

Clare asked, "Does your personal physician feel it is safe for you to fly?"

"Certainly," the old man in the expensive tweed suit snapped. "I use my company plane to visit our various branches. It brought me here from Dayton this morning."

"Of course that plane flies at much lower levels than our jets," Clare pointed out.

"You compensate for that, don't you?" he demanded.

"Yes," she agreed. "But in the event of any slight failure, you would be likely to be bothered before anyone else. You're sure your doctor approved of this flight to Hawaii?"

"Of course," he said angrily. "My condition is much better than it was at the time I had the attack. I can tell you I wouldn't want to go through an experience like that again. And the worst part was that in the beginning I felt wonderful."

"A feeling of great well-being is a first symptom of oxygen deficiency," she said describing hypoxia in simple words. "The danger is that you can experience it without realizing what is happening."

The old man showed interest. He nodded. "Just how it was with me," he asserted. "One minute I was feeling great, and the next I was in a kind of daze. My wife says I went pale, my lips and fingernails turned blue, and I started this business of trying to push open the window. I didn't even know I was on a plane. She was scared stiff."

"It must have been a terrifying experience," Clare agreed.

The important man was enjoying having her as an audience. His hawk face registered satisfaction. "Luckily, the stewardess knew what she was doing. And next thing they were giving me oxygen and telling me to lie back and breathe deeply but not too fast. It took me a while to come out of it."

"Is your wife traveling with you this time?" Clare inquired.

He looked grim again. "My wife died six months ago."

"I'm sorry," she apologized.

"All right," he said curtly. "You couldn't be expected to know."

"So you're making the flight alone?"

"Yes."

"I'll speak to the stewardess, if you don't mind," she said. "I mean for your own protection. In case there should be any emergency, she'll know something of your medical history."

The stern face showed concern. "I don't want to be fussed over!"

"Nothing like that," Clare assured him with a sympathetic smile. "But she will keep a watch on you, check from time to time to be sure you're comfortable."

"I'm perfectly well again," he insisted. "I don't need special attention."

"I understand," she said.

She at once went to her office and spoke to the stewardess on the Hawaii flight, who was still in the briefing room downstairs. Quickly she explained the situation and gave her the millionaire's name. The stewardess promised to keep a close watch on him.

They had just seen the passengers off for the Hawaii flight when others began arriving for the late afternoon jet to Dallas and Mexico City. It was while Clare was checking in the first passengers for this daily service that Isobel brought her a message.

"You're wanted on the phone," she said.

Clare nodded and hurried to her office to take the call. There were other phones in the lounge for use by passengers, but this was her private line. When she picked up the receiver, she was greeted by a male voice.

"This is McLaren in the baggage room," he said urgently. "We've had an accident here. One of the maintenance men fell from a catwalk while replacing an overhead light. Came down thirty feet onto the concrete floor. We've sent for an ambulance, but thought you might take a look and see if anything can be done while we're waiting."

"I'll be right down," she promised.

Putting down the phone, she hurried out to the lounge and told Isobel in a quiet aside there had been an accident and she'd be absent for a while. Then she rushed to the down escalator and, reaching the main floor, raced along the maze of corridors to the baggage room.

A big rawboned man in the blue working clothes of Trans-Continental's behind-the-scenes staff was waiting at the entrance of the baggage room to greet her. "I'm McLaren," he said. "I'll take you to the injured man."

Leading her by the arm, he deftly guided her past trucks loaded with freight to a spot at the far end of the big high-ceilinged shed where a knot of workers had gathered round the unfortunate maintenance man.

McLaren pushed his way through with Clare at his side. "The nurse is here!" he shouted.

The injured man was sitting up, supported by one of the freight crew.

She knelt by him. "How long ago did it happen?"

"Just a few minutes ago," the man supporting him said. "He doesn't seem to have broken any bones."

"Don't try to move him until the ambulance comes," she warned, noting the cut on the victim's head. And then, addressing herself directly to him, she asked, "Are you able to talk?"

As she expected, the words didn't reach him. She was further alarmed to notice he had some bleeding from the ears. She checked his pulse and found it rapid and weak. This alone was a sign that the man was in poor condition. His face was deathly pale, and the pupils of his eyes seemed to be unequal in size.

She told the man holding him up, "We should lower him to a level position."

The man nodded and let him down gently. McLaren had appeared with some heavy gray blankets, and she took one of them and spread it out on the hard concrete under the victim's head and shoulders. She draped another one over him.

"Maybe if he had a good shot of whiskey —" the man who had been helping suggested.

"No," she said firmly. "No stimulants."

The man stared at her anxiously. "You think he's real bad?"

She met his eyes. "He fell a long way."

The man got the message. "Yeah," he agreed. "That was some fall."

She continued to kneel beside the injured worker as they waited for the ambulance. McLaren had vanished somewhere. Suddenly she heard a commotion at the other end of the gloomy shed, and McLaren's voice was raised as he gave directions to what must be the stretcher bearers. An intern in a white uniform with a small bag in hand appeared, followed by the men with the stretcher.

He gave Clare a sharp glance as he bent over the accident victim. "What's the picture, nurse?"

"Shock, brain damage of some sort. There is bleeding from the ears."

He nodded as he examined the man under the blanket. Then he rose and told the stretcher bearers, "All right, boys. On our way." As they lifted the man onto the stretcher, he turned to Clare. "Thanks, nurse. You're right. He is in bad shape."

McLaren had followed the intern and the stretcher bearers out to the ambulance. But the big foreman came back in time to speak to Clare before she returned to her work upstairs.

His rawbone face wore an earnest look.

"Thanks for coming down so fast, Miss Andrews," he said.

"I was glad to do it," she told him.

"Poor Henry!" he sighed. "It doesn't look good for him."

"He may come through it without any trouble," she said. "The important thing was to get him under a doctor's care and in a hospital as soon as possible."

"I appreciate what you did," McLaren told her. "I hope I can return a favor for you sometime."

"It's only part of my job," she said with a faint smile as she prepared to go.

He accompanied her to the exit. "Your job is with the big shots upstairs," he said. "I had no right to bother you with our troubles."

"Any time there's an emergency, don't hesitate to call," she said.

By the time she reached the V.I.P. lounge again, the Hawaii flight had left. And the end of her day had come.

Arriving at the apartment, she found Hester there ahead of her, already preparing the evening meal. And sprawled out in an easy chair in the living room was Dick Warren, Hester's husband-to-be.

The young pilot had been reading the evening paper. Now he glanced up at Clare with a broad smile. "Hi, Nurse Andrews!" he said. "Bet you're surprised to see me!"

"I am," she admitted. "I thought you were still on the other side."

"Got back a day early," the young man said. "So I just had to come by and see you kids."

Clare smiled at him as she took off her topcoat. "Have a good trip?"

"The usual," he said, stifling a yawn. "Didn't get too much sleep." He was a sturdily built young man with a round, pleasant face and a lazy manner.

Hester, wearing an apron, presented herself in the doorway from the kitchen, looking unusually happy. "What do you think?" she asked Clare. "He's been arguing with me ever since I came home to set the wedding date ahead."

"You bet I have," Dick said from the easy chair. "I've come into a little parcel of money I didn't expect, and I can't think of a better use to put it to."

Clare just stared at him. She was thinking of the smuggling and the pilot who was being watched. To hear Dick brag about having money was something new. He was usually complaining about being broke. Where could the money have come from?

Chapter Four

Her answer came as Dick spoke again. "A friend of mine has been playing the stock market," he told them. "I gave him some cash I'd put aside, and he made a small killing for me."

"Lucky you!" Clare said with as much enthusiasm as she could muster. She had a feeling it was a thin story, but there was nothing to do but accept it at face value. She couldn't imagine Dick having the cash to invest or knowing anyone with market information.

"It's one of those breaks people get!" was Hester's happy comment. "But you can be sure it won't happen again."

Dick's round face showed a smug expression. "Don't be too sure about that," he said. "I gave him back part of what he made for me and asked him to invest it in something else. So I may have another little nest egg on the way."

This was almost too much to swallow, Clare thought angrily. He was already making up an alibi for future windfalls. Her belief that he was in on the smuggling grew every moment, and so did her fears for Hester. She said, "I thought the stock market hadn't been doing so well lately."

Dick grinned at her. "Somebody is always making money," he said. "You just have to play it right."

"I'd better get back to the meat," Hester said, laughing. "It wouldn't do to offer a big manipulator like you burned steak."

Clare slipped on an apron and went out to help her. When she was certain the kitchen door was closed between them and the young man in the living room, she asked the red-haired girl, "Are you going to let him talk you into getting married sooner than you expected to?"

Hester laughed as she worked preparing a salad in a big wooden bowl. "No. Marriage is a serious step in my family. I'm not being rushed, no matter how Dick feels about it."

Clare couldn't help giving a sigh of relief. "I think you're wise," she said.

Hester smiled at her. "Maybe Dick's friend will make him some more money while we're waiting. We might even get enough to put down the payment on a nice new house."

"That would be wonderful," Clare said,

trying to sound enthusiastic but not quite managing it. She felt Hester would be lucky if she didn't wind up seeing the young pilot led off to prison. Perhaps she was being unfair to Dick, but all the evidence pointed against him.

"What about you and Harry?" Hester asked, pausing in her work. "Have you any definite plans?"

"None."

"Can't you make your mind up between him and Boyle Heath?" Hester wanted to know.

She smiled. "They're both good friends."

"I'll bet you'll wind up turning down Harry for that actor," Hester said in a troubled voice. "And I don't like him. Anyway, he's too old!"

"Not all that old!" Clare argued.

"And he's been married twice before!"

"Boyle does live in a different kind of world from us," she admitted.

"Like the rest of the jet set in that V.I.P. lounge," Hester said with indignation. "Honestly, I don't think it's done you any good working there. You've gotten your values all twisted."

"I think its good to be exposed to how other people live," she said. "And under all his glamor, Boyle is just like anyone else.

The fact his marriages didn't work out wasn't really his fault. His first wife was a temperamental actress, and his second married him because he was a television star. He says she didn't even like him as a person."

Hester reached for a fresh loaf of French bread to begin slicing it. "Which brings up an interesting question," she said. "Just how do you separate the man from the television star? And are you sure it isn't the T.V. image you've fallen for?"

"No danger," Clare assured her friend. She busied herself pouring out glasses of tomato juice to set on the table.

They had dinner in the living room. Hester served it on the drop-leaf dining room table, which was kept discreetly against the wall when not in use. The food was good, and Dick seemed to be thoroughly enjoying himself. He dominated the conversation and kept the two girls amused.

Some of his stories were about London. "There's this place in Leicester Square," he said over coffee. "It's called 'The Guinea & The Piggy.' For a guinea, which is about two dollars and sixty cents today, you can eat as much as a piggy with a hundred and twenty dishes to choose from."

"I missed that when I was over there," Clare said.

"So did I," Hester agreed. "We should all go together sometime, and Dick could show us around. Wouldn't that be fun?"

Clare smiled. "You could go there on your honeymoon."

"No!" Dick almost shouted. "London is a working town for me. When we have our honeymoon, I'll find a real Yankee spot like good old Niagara Falls."

"Niagara Falls!" Hester protested. "That's the horse and buggy age!"

"I'm an old-fashioned guy," Dick said with one of his broad grins.

When the dinner was over, Dick invited them both to a movie. Clare tactfully refused but told them to go ahead while she did the dishes. Hester protested, but in the end did happily go out with the young pilot.

There was a light drizzle of rain the next morning. While Clare and Hester waited for the bus, they talked about the previous evening. Clare was still skeptical about Dick's explanation of his sudden windfall, but Hester seemed satisfied with his story.

"Dick is thinking about buying a new car," she said as they stood in the shelter of a store entrance watching for the bus.

"Shouldn't he wait until he sees if his good luck continues?" Clare said.

"He seems to think it will," Hester said.

"I've never known him to be so confident. But then you know how reckless he is about money and things generally."

"I know," Clare agreed.

The bus finally came, and so their discussion ended. Isobel already had the morning lists of arrivals and departures by the time Clare changed into her neat blue uniform and reported for duty in the V.I.P. lounge.

"The weather isn't bad enough to delay any flights," Isobel told her as she gave her copies of the mimeographed sheets with the passengers' names.

"I didn't think it would be," Clare said, scanning the lists quickly. Then, giving her attention to the stewardess again, she noticed the blonde girl looked pale and tense. "How are things at home?" she asked.

Isobel gave her a resigned look. "Not too good," she said. "Mother had a poor night. I didn't get much sleep."

"You look tired," Clare agreed. "Why didn't you call in and take the day off? You have to get your rest."

"I'll be all right," the other girl said. "My work here isn't that hard."

"But it does put a strain on your nerves," Clare said. "And that's difficult when you're already weary."

The morning flights going out were not

too heavily booked, so this did make their work easier. But there were several cases where passengers arrived in from overseas points and transferred to flights to other parts of North and South America. A Professor Vincent Carlos and his attractive dark-eyed daughter were among this group. He was a withered man in his sixties with an excitable manner and haggard features. In contrast, his daughter was in her early twenties, stylish and beautiful. The old man was president of a university in Brazil, and they were returning from an international meeting of college heads in Paris.

The old man seemed shaky and on the verge of collapse as he approached Clare and complained about the long wait he and his daughter had to face before their plane left for Rio de Janeiro. "Most upsetting," he told her emphatically. "We were given to understand there would be only an hour's delay."

His daughter clung to his arm and reminded him, "But, Father, the agent downstairs explained it all to you. The schedules have recently been changed."

The professor continued to be enraged. "They should have explained that to us before we left Paris," he said. "We could have taken another flight."

"Probably they hadn't received the latest information," Clare said. "You will find that time passes quickly. We have good restaurants in the terminal. Or I can have you served in a private dining room up here if you'd prefer."

Professor Carlos was not to be placated. "I would prefer to be on my way," he said severely.

His daughter gave Clare an embarrassed look. "My father is not well," she explained. "The trip has been very difficult for him."

"It would be wise for you to relax, professor," Clare warned him, not liking his ashen look or the trembling clearly visible in his hands. "We'll do all we can to make you comfortable."

The old man gave the impression he was going to offer her another angry reply, but instead he suddenly seemed to stiffen, and there was an expression of panic on his haggard face. Then he slumped quickly to the carpeted floor at their feet. His daughter screamed, and Clare knelt down to aid him.

"My father!" the girl moaned in her lightly accented English.

"He's breathing," Clare told her to allay any fears she might have that he had died instantly. It was true he was still alive, but his breathing was shallow and difficult. His mouth was drawn down on one side. It took her only a moment to diagnose that the professor had suffered an attack of apoplexy.

Isobel had now joined them. The blonde girl asked, "What is it?"

"He's had a stroke," Clare told her quietly. "He's a hospital case, an emergency. Call an ambulance."

As Isobel rushed away to carry out her instructions, Clare gently moved the patient on his back. She told his daughter, "Bring me a pillow from one of the divans."

The dark girl quickly got one and brought it to her. Clare placed it under the professor's shoulders so that his head was slightly raised. The old man's breathing seemed to falter for an instant, and Clare trembled for fear he might have died. But then the laborious gasping resumed.

His daughter was close to hysteria. "My father! Will he live?"

Clare got to her feet and touched the girl's arm in sympathy. "He has had a stroke. His condition is serious, but there's every chance he will recover with proper hospital care. An ambulance is on its way."

Isobel returned. "They're coming," she said. "Anything else?"

"Yes," Clare said. "Get me some cold cloths and a bucket of ice."

She spent the time until the ambulance came applying the cold cloths to the old man's head. After he was taken to the hospital, with the girl accompanying him in the ambulance, the lounge settled down to something like normal again. But Clare was far behind in her morning's work and felt the strain of the ordeal she'd gone through.

When she went down to the cafeteria, she found she had no appetite. So instead of her regular lunch, she settled for a cup of black coffee. Harry had left for England on one of his frequent business trips for the air line, so she could not expect to see him. Finding an unoccupied table, she sat alone, feeling dejected and letdown.

She was reviewing the hectic morning in her mind when a familiar voice spoke her name. She looked up and saw it was the foreman of the baggage shed, McLaren, who stood there.

"I don't mean to interrupt, Miss Andrews," he said apologetically. "But I figured you'd be glad to know that Henry is coming around all right."

Clare smiled. "That's the best news I've had this morning. I was worried about him. He seemed badly hurt."

"He was," the foreman agreed. "But the

doctors say he responded well to treatment and he'll recover."

"Good," she said. "That was a long distance to fall."

"I don't know how he came to lose his footing," McLaren said. "He's an experienced man. But I guess it could happen to anyone."

"We've never been able to eliminate accidents completely," she agreed. "Otherwise you wouldn't be needing me here."

"And it's a good thing you are here," the big man said. "I never appreciated that more than when Henry fell." With a nod he moved out of the cafeteria.

Clare felt better for the few words with him. Finishing her coffee, she left the cafeteria and went out to the main waiting room. There was the usual flow of people, the profusion of luggage with labels from all over the world, the regular harsh bleating of flight departures and arrivals. The melancholy drizzle of the dark day seemed to have somehow seeped into the big room, giving it a cold, damp air. This was the less glamorous side of air travel as compared with the luxury of her own domain, the V.I.P. lounge.

She was about to continue to take the escalator upstairs when she saw a familiar

68

figure in a dark trench coat coming across to meet her. It was the television star, Boyle Heath, back from London. He wore his usual charming smile, but she noticed that he was limping ever so slightly as he came toward her.

"Clare!" he said. "What luck! I was going up to find you, and you've saved me the trouble." He gave her a quick kiss on the right cheek. "What a rotten day to come back home."

She smiled. "It is miserable. And you're limping. What's wrong?"

"Oh, that," he said very casually. "It's an old leg injury. Gives me some trouble when the weather is damp. Dates back to an accident I had in Switzerland too many years ago."

Clare looked up into the handsome face, still youthful in spite of some telltale lines at the corners of the eyes and around the mouth.

She said, "You always try to pretend you're ages old."

"I am," he said. "That's why your youth appeals to me so. Did you miss me?"

"I always do," she said. "How did the tapings go?"

"The usual problems." He sighed. "But we finished on schedule, which was somewhat miraculous. Where are we going to have dinner tonight?"

She laughed. "I wasn't aware that we were having it anywhere."

"But we are," he said. "How about the Chateau Richelieu? We haven't been there for a long time."

"Oughtn't you rest?" she asked, giving him a concerned appraisal. "You must be tired."

"Now you're making me feel old," he teased her. "I've been looking forward to seeing you. Where will we meet?"

"At the restaurant," she suggested. "I'll take the subway in and then a cab. That will make it easier for you."

"If you insist," he said. "I've got some things to do: see my agent and all that kind of nonsense. I'll take you home by cab. We can go dancing at the Barberry Room after dinner. It's near the Richelieu."

She gave him a reproving smile. "With that troublesome leg of yours?"

"Don't worry about it," he said. "It ought to be better by tonight."

"Unless it is, we'll forget about dancing," she said. "I enjoy just sitting and talking."

"We can decide later," he said. "Just now I'm anxious to get into town and take care of my appointments. I'll move on to the cab stand."

He walked with her to the escalator, and then they parted.

By careful timing Clare caught the subway and then picked up a taxi on Sixth Avenue to take her to the Chateau Richelieu. When she got there it was just a few minutes past eight, and Boyle Heath was seated at the bar waiting for her.

He came to greet her, looking suave in a dark suit and black bow tie. "I have our table reserved and your favorite rosé ordered," he told her. He picked up his drink as they passed the bar and took it with him as the headwaiter led them to a quiet corner table.

She liked the intimate French restaurant with its elegant crimson decor. She ordered her favorite items from the menu: vichyssoise, filet of sole and Brussels sprouts. It was a delicious meal, and they lingered over it right up to the demitasse and crème de menthe.

Clare smiled at him dreamily across the table. "I don't think you can get better food than this anywhere in the world."

"I'm inclined to agree," he said. "I have some favorite spots in London, but none better than this place."

Clare sighed. "What a strange life I lead."

"Meaning?" The actor arched an eyebrow.

"It just occurred to me that I'm sort of a split personality," she said. "For eight hours a day I'm surrounded by the luxury of the V.I.P. lounge. I enjoy the atmosphere, even if I'm just an employee. Then I go back to my very ordinary apartment and my very ordinary world." She paused to smile at him. "Except for the time I spend with you. You transport me back to the world of glamor and luxury again."

Boyle studied her with an air of great sincerity. "This could be your world all the time if you'd just say the word."

She laughed. "Please don't try to confuse me completely."

"I mean it," he said seriously. "You have the beauty and intelligence to fit in anywhere."

"Being with you gives me confidence," she said.

"I'm glad it does," he said with a touch of bitterness. "For sometimes I think I lack that quality myself." He paused. "Something happened today that will make a big difference to me."

She sensed he was deeply disturbed, in spite of the casual way he spoke. She asked, "What is it, Boyle?"

He looked straight at her with troubled eyes. "My agent told me this afternoon the show isn't being renewed. When the thirteen weeks are up, I'll be finished."

"That's awful!" she said. "And you're so good in it."

He smiled ruefully. "Too good, so my agent tells me. He says the show is too sophisticated for mass audiences."

"But you'll be sure to get another show!"

He shook his head. "Don't count on it. When you get a bad rating in television, no one wants to touch you. Of course I can always look for a Broadway play."

"But that's so risky," she protested. "I mean, often a good show closes after one week."

"I know," he said. And with a brighter smile: "Thank Heavens there is always London. I have the promise of several independent one-hour television plays over there. They don't pay as well, but it will mean regular money coming in."

"But you'll have the expense of traveling," she said, "unless you stay over there."

"I won't do that," he said. "I'll have to try to work on a new program for over here." He hesitated. "And I don't want to be separated from you."

"I can't mean that much to you," she told him.

"Let me prove it," he said gravely. "And

you can prove something as well: that you care for me and not the television star. I'm at a low ebb in my career right now and not so young any more. Knowing I'm out of work, or almost, would you consider marrying me?"

Before she realized what she was saying, she said, "Your losing the show doesn't make any difference."

To her confusion, he took her words as an acceptance. "I'll get your ring in the morning," he promised.

Chapter Five

For a moment Clare was certain he didn't mean her to take his words seriously. But then she saw the sober expression on his face and knew his proposal had been in earnest. She was completely surprised and didn't know what to say. She had no desire to hurt him or lose his friendship, yet she knew she couldn't let him assume she'd accepted him.

As a stopgap she said, "There's no hurry."

"I like to get things settled," he said with a smile. Glancing at his watch, he added, "It's time we move on to the Barberry Room if we're going to do any dancing."

"Are you certain your leg is well enough?"

"Positive. Didn't you notice? I'm walking with hardly any limp now. I took a warm bath before dressing for the evening, and all the stiffness in my knee vanished."

Clare was still feeling uneasy, worried about the wrong impression she seemed to have given him. She said, "I'll have to be home fairly early. I report for work at eight."

"Ghastly hour!" He smiled. "The only time I was ever up that early was when I spent a few months in Hollywood doing a movie. They make you begin work at dawn there, and travel to some distant location as well. It means getting up in the middle of the night. I often think that explains a lot of the poor films they turn out. Who can act decently at that hour of the morning?"

She laughed. "Maybe you should try Hollywood again. The early rising would do you good."

"Not me," he assured her. "And anyway, they're doing mostly second-rate television films out there. Nothing I'd be interested in." He called the waiter over and asked for their bill.

They walked the short block up Fifty-second Street to the Barberry Room, which was on the opposite side of the street in the Berkshire Hotel. As they strolled along in the darkness, Boyle complained of the poor job his agent had done for him and the problems he would face in finding another series show. She listened politely, even though her mind was occupied with other thoughts.

She had decided that before they left the Barberry Room she would make it plain that she could not accept his ring, that she wasn't ready to become engaged to anyone yet. If she let the evening go by without doing this, she would be bound to regret it and she wouldn't be able to sleep. It would mean waiting for the precise moment when it would be best to break the news and hoping he'd take it the right way.

The Barberry Room was well-filled with dinner and dance patrons. The headwaiter recognized Boyle and greeted him by name before leading them to a table near the dance floor in the long room with its candy-striped red and white decor.

The orchestra was good, and Boyle took her on the floor at once. He was a good dancer, and Clare found herself enjoying the evening so much she almost forgot about the misunderstanding she still had to clear up. Some of the other dancers apparently recognized Boyle Heath. There were furtive whispers among them and shy glances in their direction from time to time. Clare was amused that they seemed so awed by the handsome television star, and she enjoyed being seen in his company.

As eleven o'clock came and she knew she must leave within a few minutes, she brought up the subject of their engagement. Studying him across their table, she said, "Boyle, there is one thing I must clear up."

He'd been giving his attention to the orchestra, which had resumed with a South American medley. Tapping his fingers lightly on the table, he glanced at her with a smile. "What's that?"

"I can't accept a ring from you."

"Isn't that the customary procedure for an engaged couple?"

She smiled wearily. "That's the whole point. We can't become an engaged couple. At least not yet."

He let his brow furrow. "I seem to remember you saying yes when we were across the street."

"You tricked me into it," she said with a sigh. "Or at least you misunderstood me."

He smiled a faint smile. "Suppose you think it over. And tomorrow I'll bring the diamond along anyway, in the hope you've changed your mind."

"Please don't," she begged.

"I'd like to have lunch with you at the airport," he said as if he hadn't heard her. "I'd enjoy taking a tour of the place. I've always had an interest in the control tower of a big airport. Could you take me behind the scenes?"

"I suppose so."

Boyle Heath had turned on all his charm. "Then tomorrow noon I'll expect the guided tour. You can get a little extra time off, can't you?"

"Yes, if nothing unexpected happens. We had a bad day today, so the law of averages should assure us of an uneventful tomorrow."

The actor said, "Let's have one more dance before I take you home." And they got up to join the others on the small floor.

He took her home in a taxi, and his last words after kissing her good night at the door were that he'd be on hand for lunch. She went into the silence of the darkened apartment, full of doubts and fears. She had enjoyed the evening, but she was worried about him visiting her at lunch time. She could imagine the attention he'd get in the staff cafeteria and the gossip that would follow.

The weather was favorable, if that was any portent. When she reported for work in the V.I.P. lounge the following morning, the sun was streaming in through its glass walls.

She spoke to Isobel about taking a long lunch hour. "Do you think you can manage until I get back?" she asked.

The blonde girl smiled. "Of course I can," she said. "I may have to ask you the same kind of favor next week."

"Any time," Clare told her.

"Mother is going into the hospital on Monday," Isobel explained. "She's having another operation. I'd like to go to the hospital whichever day it is scheduled."

"You should take the full day off," Clare suggested.

The blonde girl sighed. "No. I'd rather not do that. It would give me too much time to mope around and worry. But I would like to call in briefly and see her or at least get a personal report on her condition."

"You seem more rested," Clare said. "You must have gotten a better sleep last night."

"I did," Isobel said, her eyes bright. The neat blue uniform and cap suited her milky complexion and slim figure. "Mother seemed much better. I'm hoping another operation will see her out of trouble."

"Do the doctors think so?"

Isobel's happy look dimmed. "They say it's the only thing. She has to have it." And then, changing the subject, she passed the passenger lists to Clare, saying, "We don't seem to have so many heavily booked flights today."

She took them and skimmed over them quickly. "I wonder how Professor Carlos is," she mused as she studied the sheets.

"I haven't any idea what hospital they took him to," Isobel said. "I'll try to find out."

The first to gather in the V.I.P. lounge were a group of passengers for the West Coast flight. Many of these were repeaters whose business kept them commuting between the East and West. They were familiar with the routine of the lounge and gave little trouble. Settling down with favorite papers or magazines, they accepted the coffee or drinks offered them and waited for the announcement they could board their plane.

One of the familiars, a tycoon in the oil business, greeted Clare with a grim smile when he entered the lounge. "I'm feeling under the weather," he told her.

"But you're never ill!" she protested.

"I'm not ill now," he said. "But I do have a hangover. And I've got to study reports the entire flight." He lifted a bulging brief case as proof of this. "You have anything to help?"

"I'll fix you up something right away," she promised. And she went into her office to mix the effervescent saline remedy that was standard in such cases. As she stirred it, she smiled wryly to herself. Harry would indict her again for this kind of nursing. She wondered how the busy young executive was making out in London. It would be well along in the day there at this moment.

Her phone rang, and she answered it. She recognized the voice of Arnold Benson's prim secretary as the girl said, "Mr. Benson would like to see you at once."

"Very well," she said. "I'll be there as soon as I give some medicine to a passenger." Replacing the phone, she hurried out to the lounge and gave the oil tycoon the saline drink. He accepted it with thanks and was sipping it when she left.

Arnold Benson motioned her to sit down as soon as she entered his large office. He was seated behind his desk and made no move to get up. "I wanted to find out if you'd noticed anything out of the way," he said, "and also to let you know the Federal men report another shipment of stolen gems have been delivered in New York."

She said, "I was talking with René Le Blanc."

The austere, bald man raised his bushy gray eyebrows. "Indeed? Why didn't you report this to me? You know he is one of the suspects."

"I wasn't sure the conversation had any importance."

"You don't have to decide that," he told her in a vexed tone. "All I ask is that you report such incidents to me."

"I'm sorry," she said. "He was leaving for

London. And he did mention that he'd like to have a chat with me when he came back."

Arnold Benson frowned. "Are you two old friends?"

"No." She shook her head. "I had barely spoken to him before. But the other day he was very friendly. He spoke of having some job in mind for me, something that would pay better than what I'm doing."

"But this sounds as if he's ready to enlist you as an accomplice," the general manager said, leaning forward on the desk, his eyes keen with interest. "If he approaches you when he returns from London, I'll count on you encouraging him to explain his proposition."

"I planned on doing that."

"Very good, Miss Andrews," the bald man said. "I believe you have made a promising start. Remember Le Blanc, Gloria Faith and Fritz Manner are the three the Federal men have their eyes on."

Clare said, "What about our own employees? Didn't you mention there was a pilot under suspicion?"

Arnold Benson looked wary. "Perhaps I did," he said in a dry tone. "It follows that some of our staff have to be involved in an operation as big as this one."

"They're bound to be rounded up, aren't they?" she asked.

The bald executive mistook her interest for fear. "Don't you worry on that score," he said crisply. "I'll guarantee they'll be brought to justice. And you needn't worry about being harmed by any of them."

"René Le Blanc travels back and forth a good deal," she said.

"So do Gloria Faith and Fritz Manner," the man behind the desk said. "And we've discovered that the pattern of the stolen jewel shipments almost match their arrivals in this country. So you see our investigation is based on solid fact."

"There are other people who go overseas quite often," Clare said. "Boyle Heath, for one."

"The television star," Arnold Benson said. "Of course he has a good reason for doing so. I believe he does most of his shows in London." He stood up. "That will be all for the moment, Miss Andrews. But in the future come to me at once with any information concerning those three. Will you remember?"

"I'll remember, sir," Clare promised as she also got to her feet.

She'd barely arrived back in the lounge before another group of passengers arrived.

She and Isobel were kept busy attending to their needs until almost noon. Then a smiling Boyle Heath appeared in the doorway of the lounge.

Going across to him, she said, "You're right on time."

"I intended to be," he told her. "Any place where we can be alone for a few minutes before we go down to eat?"

"My office," she said. "Excuse me while I let Isobel know I'm leaving." This attended to, she led him into her office. He didn't say a word, but took a velvet box from his jacket pocket and opened it to reveal a huge, sparkling diamond ring. Clare gasped at its size. "You brought it after all."

"Try it on for size," he said, taking it from the box.

"No!" she said in near panic. "Please put it away."

"You promised."

"I didn't," she argued. "And if you make a big issue of it, I won't even have lunch with you."

The handsome actor looked disappointed. "You sound as if you mean that."

"I do."

He gave a deep sigh and, returning the ring to its box, replaced it in his pocket. "We can discuss it later, then," he said.

"We understand each other now," Clare said firmly.

"Surely I'm entitled to a kiss at least," he said, "for coming way out here."

"You came out for a tour of the control tower," she reminded him.

He laughed. "Let's call the kiss part of the guided tour," he said, and took her in his arms without allowing her any further protests.

This meant repairing her lipstick before she went downstairs with him. She knew she was blushing furiously as they passed Isobel at the lounge door on their way out.

On the down escalator, Boyle Heath said, "Who's the other girl? She seems nice."

"She is," Clare agreed. "And she has a big problem: a sick mother who isn't apt to get better."

"Sorry to hear that," the actor said with a note of genuine sympathy in his voice. "She's much too young and pretty to have that kind of responsibility."

"Some people are more willing to shoulder responsibility than others," Clare told him.

"Don't look at me when you say that," Boyle teased. "I offer to marry you, and look at the way I'm treated."

She made no reply to this but led him to

the cafeteria. It was busy, as usual, and the sight of the handsome television star in the line with his tray caused a good deal of excitement in the big room. Two of the elderly women from the accounts division went so far as to come up to their table with giggling requests for autographs. Clare knew that before the end of the day everyone at Trans-Continental would be linking her name with Boyle's. And Harry would be in a rage about it when he came back and heard.

As the buxom females from accounts retreated with their autographs, Boyle smiled at her. "It seems I'm still pretty popular," he said.

"You know you are."

"I may not be in a few months after the show ends," he said grimly. "People have short memories."

"I can't believe you'd be forgotten that quickly," she protested.

"I could name you a half-dozen stars who were household names and whom no one thinks of now," he assured her. "It's a matter of exposure."

She offered a smile of encouragement. "You'll get another series, I'm sure."

"I'd better," he said.

"And we'd better be on our way if you

want to look around and visit the control towers," she said.

They left the Trans-Continental building and walked out into the bright sunshine. Not far away were the buildings of Pan-American, TWA and another big terminal housing a half-dozen of the foreign air lines.

Boyle's hair was ruffled by the breeze as he glanced around, shading his eyes from the sunlight with his hand. "I always get a thrill out of this airport," he said.

"Kennedy is one of the busiest in the world," she agreed.

She hailed one of the Trans-Continental service trucks and got them a swift ride to the main control tower. They took an elevator to the big room at the top known as the "cab," whose slanting glass walls permitted a clear view of the whole of the vast airport. Here the traffic controllers worked with microphones in front of them and earphones clamped to their heads.

A tall, friendly-looking man in shirt sleeves with his collar open and his tie hanging loosely knotted around it came over to them. He grinned at Clare. "Well, Miss Trans-Continental," he said, "are you here to find out if we're taking good care of your planes?"

She shook her head. "No. I promised to

show Boyle the tower." And she introduced the star to the communications man, whose first name was Joe.

Boyle was plainly impressed. "All this is a bit beyond me," he admitted.

"It's pretty complicated," Joe agreed. "Gets more so every day."

He showed Boyle the tower with the radar sail that never stopped spinning. "That picks up signals from planes within range and transmits them in the form of little specks of light to the radar-scope downstairs," he said.

Boyle said, "I'm always shocked at the noise jets make."

Joe nodded. "The mechanics and ground service men wear steel-plated earmuffs to protect their hearing. And if you're ever close to a jet when it's getting ready to take off, get as far away as you can as fast as you can and put your fingers in your ears."

Clare laughed. "I found out about that one day after I was nearly deafened."

Boyle gazed out the glass walls at the runways. "Just how are the runways planned?" he asked.

"They're angled to take advantage of the prevailing winds," Joe told him, "and numbered according to magnetic headings. That's measured in degrees clockwise from the magnetic North Pole. The pilot adds a zero to the runway number and allows for the deviation you find in every compass. If he's heading for runway 28 at any airport, he knows the compass should indicate about 280 degrees magnetic."

"What happens when the weather closes in?" Boyle wanted to know.

Joe shrugged. "They use the instrument landing runway. Has broken lines down the middle and eight solid lines to make its edges. At one end of this runway a building houses the glide-path transmitter which sends out radio signals to guide the pilot when he can't see the ground. At the far end of the runway there's the localizer that activates a device in the plane's cockpit. By watching it, the pilot can guide in his craft on the exact center of the runway."

Clare smiled at Boyle. "See. You needn't worry any more when you come back here in the fog."

"I'll still worry," he assured them. And to Joe, "One thing that makes me wonder is how so many planes can travel up there without running into one another."

"They do that once in a while," Joe said with a thin smile, "but not often. We have Federal airways, a network of electronic freeways, each ten miles wide, extending the length and breadth of the country and invisible except for maps. The routes are used on three levels, low altitudes for slow aircraft and short flights, medium for faster aircraft, and the 20,000 foot altitude where the jets begin."

"And I suppose the ocean air lanes are divided the same way?" Boyle asked.

"Pretty much," Joe said. "The I.A.T.A. and the I.C.A.O. make the rules for overseas travel and see that they aren't violated."

Boyle looked around at the battery of radio telephones, teletype machines and the intent men manning them. He smiled. "It's lived up to my expectations," he said.

They left the control tower, and Clare was lucky enough to recognize the driver of a service car belonging to Pan-American. She hailed him, and he took them back to the entrance of the Trans-Continental terminal. She glanced at her watch and saw that she was nearly an hour overdue for work.

"It's getting late," she said. "I'll really have to report back to the lounge."

Boyle smiled. "That was fun."

"I enjoyed it myself," she said.

The actor hesitated. "What about the ring?"

She shook her head. "My decision still goes."

"You're spoiling my day," he warned.

Clare gave him a teasing look. "You're just saying that."

"I mean it."

"We'll talk about it again. I have to go now."

Boyle looked romantically rueful and clung to her arm. "When will I see you again?"

"You can call me."

"I will," he promised. And he touched his lips to her cheek before allowing her to go.

She said, "I'm in uniform!"

"It didn't spoil the kiss," he laughed as she left him to go inside.

Isobel was waiting for her when she entered the lounge. The blonde girl seemed nervous. She said, "I'm glad you're here. A call just came for you from downstairs. They want you to call back."

"Who was it?" Clare asked.

"A stewardess from the flight that just came in from London," Isobel said. "Her name is Moore. She's in their dressing room. And she said it was urgent."

Chapter Six

Clare found it hard to imagine what the call might be about, but she lost no time entering her office and asking to be put through to the extension number left by the stewardess. After a moment a girl answered the phone, and Clare asked to speak with Miss Moore.

"If you'll hold the line a minute," the girl said, "I'll try to get her."

Clare waited what seemed a long time. Finally someone at the other end picked up the phone, and a harried female voice asked, "Is that Nurse Andrews?"

"Yes. You left a message for me?"

"I certainly did." The girl's tone was fretful and indignant. "I'm in a terrible fix down here. I came in on the London plane. One of our passengers has been giving us a lot of trouble. Ordinarily she'd have been sent up to the V.I.P. lounge, but she was in such bad shape when I took her off the plane I brought her to an anteroom off our quarters down here."

Clare frowned as she listened to this dismal story. "What's wrong? Is this woman ill?"

"Ill!" the stewardess said angrily. "I suppose you could say so. The truth is she's been drinking and taking some kind of barbiturates. She's in a half-drugged and drunken state. And she's due in Chicago for a concert tonight. She was supposed to take the next plane out. It's Gloria Faith."

"Gloria Faith!" Clare echoed the name of the famed one-time movie star. The pieces all fitted together in her mind. Not only was Gloria Faith one of those under suspicion as a jewel smuggler; she was also known to be on the downgrade in her profession chiefly because of her drinking. Lately she'd been touring under the management of an ex-husband, doing personal concert appearances, cashing in on a voice that no longer really existed.

"I don't know what to do," the girl downstairs wailed. "She keeps asking about the Chicago plane. But I can't take the responsibility of putting her on it. That's why I've called you."

"Is she alone?" Clare asked. She couldn't imagine that the star would be. Even a fading actress such as Gloria Faith was not apt to travel without a personal manager or companion.

94

"Her ex-husband was with her," Stewardess Moore said unhappily. "But they fought the whole way across the Atlantic and when the plane landed and she wasn't able to stand up, he walked out on her, leaving her on my hands!"

"Is she better now?"

"I was finally able to get her on her feet, but she's still not fit to travel alone."

"It's a decision for someone higher than us to make," Clare told the girl. "I'll try and get through to Mr. Benson. As soon as I get some instructions from him I'll be right down."

"I wish you'd hurry," the stewardess said. "I'm off duty now, and I don't much care hanging around catering to this female alcoholic."

"I won't lose any time," Clare promised. And she hung up. Then she picked up the phone again and asked to be put through to Arnold Benson's office. The prim secretary answered first and, hearing that Clare's message was urgent, let her speak with Trans-Continental's great man.

Clare quickly told him the facts. She finished by saying, "It doesn't seem she's fit to travel to Chicago by herself."

"I see," Benson's dry tones came over the line. "She wouldn't have to leave for a while to be in time for an eight-thirty curtain. She could rest three or four hours until she's in better shape and then take a Chicago flight."

"Her mind is so fogged I don't think she could be counted on to work that out alone," Clare told him.

"I didn't think she would be able to do it," Benson said with some acerbity. "You will remain with her and take care of her."

Clare was stunned. "But what about my work here in the lounge?"

"I'll send an extra stewardess up there to help the other young woman while you're occupied with Miss Faith," Arnold Benson said. "You must realize this is a tremendously important matter to the line. This Faith woman is one of the smuggling suspects. It's possible that you may pick up some valuable information while you're with her."

"I understand, sir," Clare said. "You want me to look after her until she is on the plane to Chicago."

"Not at all," he snapped. "I want you to go to Chicago with her and deliver her to the theatre where she is to appear. It might be a good idea for you to try to win her confidence."

The project was getting bigger and more involved every moment.

She said, "What will I do with her? She's

in a room off the lounge used by the stewardess staff downstairs."

"I'll send my limousine around to the side entrance," Benson told her. "You bring Miss Faith out to it. Meanwhile I'll make a reservation for you at the International Motel, which is on the airport grounds. My limousine will call again when it is time for you to take the late afternoon flight and deliver you back here."

"I'll do my best," Clare said weakly.

"I'll expect no less from you," Arnold Benson said in his severe manner. "And if there are any snarl-ups, any problems at all during the afternoon, don't hesitate to get in touch with me. I'll book you and Miss Faith for a five o'clock flight to Chicago. That ought barely to give you time."

"Yes, sir," she said.

"Leave everything in my hands," the general manager of Trans-Continental told her. "For a start, I'll see the limousine is waiting for you."

Clare put down the phone in a bewildered state. The quick instructions snapped out by the austere company head had left her dazed. But she realized she had no time to stand there feeling sorry for herself. Arnold Benson was expecting fast action from her, and so fast action she must offer.

Her first step was to go outside and inform Isobel of the problem that had come up. "Mr. Benson is sending someone to assist you," she told her. "I may not get back for a couple of days."

Isobel looked astounded. "Does he expect you to leave town just as you are?"

"I guess so," she said resignedly. "There are shops at the Chicago airport and probably at the hotel. I can pick up a nightie and a change of underthings. There won't be time for me to go back to the apartment and pack."

"I think Mr. Benson is unreasonable," Isobel declared.

"Of course he is," Clare said with a tired smile. "But what can I do about it?"

"What about your girl friend? The one you share the apartment with?"

"I'll call her before I leave," Clare said. "And I'll phone you if there's any change of plan."

Leaving Isobel, she went directly downstairs to the lounge used by the girls in the stewardess department. The Moore girl turned out to be in her late twenties, a brunette with good looks marred only by frown furrows in her forehead. She had changed from her uniform to a smart brown suit.

"Well?" she asked.

"I'm to take her to the International Motel," Clare told her.

"Lucky you!" the girl said wryly. She jerked her head. "She's in the first room on the right. I leave her all to you."

"Hadn't you better come and introduce me?" Clare asked.

"No need," the other girl said. "I told her you were coming." And she went out.

Clare had no chance to argue the point. With some reluctance she made her way to the closed door of the anteroom and, after knocking gently on it, opened it and stepped inside. The sight that met her eyes was not promising. Gloria Faith was curled up on a cot which, with a chair and a small table, made up the room's only furniture. She had her back turned to Clare and was gathered up in a forlorn, disheveled heap.

Clare went over to her and touched her gently on the shoulder. "Are you ready to leave, Miss Faith?"

The figure remained motionless until Clare repeated her question in a louder voice. Then Gloria Faith stirred and glanced up at her. Clare was shocked by the pale, lined face of the once lovely star. Gloria Faith had deteriorated greatly even in the short time since Clare had last seen her. The dark-haired woman's large green eyes were glazed as she raised herself on an elbow.

"Time to leave for Chicago?" she asked in a blurred voice. "Where's Ben?"

Clare knew that Ben was her ex-husband and wasn't likely to appear after the battle they'd had. She said, "I'm going to be with you. And we're moving to a motel here at the airport first to freshen up and get ready for the flight to Chicago."

"Sounds good," Gloria Faith said in a thick voice. "I feel awful."

"A rest and cold shower will help you," Clare promised as she mentally reviewed a plan to attempt to get the star in some kind of shape.

The dark woman searched on the cot until she located a large black straw handbag that matched the stylish outfit she was wearing. "I've got some pills here," she said, slurring her words.

Clare warded off her attempt to open the bag. "I'd say you've already had more than enough pills," she said.

Gloria Faith looked up at her sullenly. "You sound like Ben!"

"Please get up," Clare pleaded. "There's a car waiting for us, and we haven't too much time."

"Got to get that plane. Concert tonight,"

the star said, making a motion to rise and wobbling back. Clare quickly grasped her arm and helped her to a standing position.

"Do you think you can walk if I help you?" she asked.

Gloria Faith drew herself up indignantly, looking ridiculous in her wrinkled clothes. "I can walk by myself," she said. "I'll show you."

She tried but after a moment was glad to lean on Clare. Somehow they got out to the waiting limousine. The driver assisted Clare with the unstable Gloria Faith both there and when they arrived at the motel. Arnold Benson had made all arrangements for their registration, and they were immediately whisked up to a room reserved in Clare's name. When they were alone at last, she drew a sigh of relief.

Gloria Faith, sprawled in an easy chair, announced, "I think I'm going to be sick."

And she was. Clare felt it was a good thing. It helped get rid of the poisons with which the star had filled her stomach. Clare gave her a simple sedative to quiet her nerves and enable her to get a couple of hours' sound sleep.

Sitting up in bed, Gloria Faith's pale face showed curiosity. "I've seen you some place before."

Clare smiled. "You've seen me many times. I'm the nurse in the V.I.P. lounge."

"Sure!" Gloria Faith said. "That's where I've met you." Her expression changed to one of disgust. "That Ben deserted me! The rat wants to see me fall down on my contract."

"If you'll just rest now," Clare begged, "I'll call you in plenty of time to have a shower and dress before we leave."

The star showed interest. "You're going to Chicago with me?"

"Yes. The air line wants to be sure you get there on time."

Gloria Faith seemed impressed. "That's what I call good service. I like you, Clare Andrews!"

"Thanks."

"Be sure my bags get on the plane," the star told her. "I couldn't go on without my costumes."

"I'll look after them," Clare promised.

"I do a full dozen changes in the show," Gloria Faith went on. "I like to give them their money's worth." She raised a dainty hand to her mouth as she yawned.

"If you want to get the full benefit of that sedative, you should try to sleep," Clare said. "I'll be in the next room reading."

"Sure," Gloria Faith said. And then she looked around. "Where's my bag?"

"Over here," Clare said. She went to the dresser and got the black straw bag. It was large and shiny and made with a long shoulder strap so it could be looped over one shoulder like a binocular case. Handing the bag to the star, she said, "You seem to worry a lot about this."

"I do," the woman in bed said, taking the bag. She opened it, took a number of items out of it and deposited them on the bed-spread. And then, to Clare's astonishment, she reached into the shiny bag and seemed to manipulate something. The next minute she dumped the bag upside down, and a string of pearls, a diamond necklace and matching bracelet and a number of other rich-looking items of jewelry, including several rings, showered out of it. She glanced up and said nonchalantly, "I just wanted to make sure Ben hadn't helped himself to these."

Clare stared at the jewels. "You always carry them with you?" she asked.

"Why not?" the star asked. "I use them for my shows, and they're insured."

"But in your handbag?"

"What better place for them?" Gloria Faith asked as she replaced the jewels in the big handbag and then closed the false bottom before refilling it with the more usual items for such a bag. When she'd finished, she passed it back to Clare. "You take care of this while I'm asleep."

Clare took the handbag. "I don't like to be responsible."

"I told you they were insured," Gloria Faith said in a tired voice. "I just don't want the nuisance of some maid helping herself to a ring or two and causing me a lot of trouble. Now let me get that shut-eye!"

With mixed feelings, Clare drew the curtains of the bedroom. Then, leaving the star in near darkness, she went quietly out to the living room of the motel suite.

Waiting until she was certain the star was asleep, she went to the phone and carefully dialed the Trans-Continental terminal on an outside line. There was an exasperating wait before she was put through to Arnold Benson.

The general manager sounded querulous. "Well, Miss Andrews?"

"I had to call you, Mr. Benson," she said. "I think I've an important lead on the jewel smuggling.

"Oh?" He sounded interested.

She told him quickly in a low voice, leaving out none of the details. "Miss Faith is asleep and shouldn't wake up for an hour or more."

"Fine," the general manager said. "One of the Federal men working on the case is right here at the terminal. I'll send him over, and you can show him that bag and what is in it."

"If it should be smuggled goods, will we still plan to go to Chicago?" she asked.

"I can't answer you," he told her. "The Federal man will decide that. I'll get him to the motel as fast as I can. His name is Munson."

She put down the phone and tiptoed over to the bedroom door, but there was no sound from inside.

At last there was a soft knock on the door of the suite. She quickly went over and opened it to allow a middle-aged, stocky man to enter. He doffed his soft hat to reveal a head of close-cropped gray hair and a square, determined face.

"I'm Munson," he said. "Arnold Benson sent me."

"I know," she said breathlessly. And with a fearful glance toward the inner door, "I only hope Miss Faith remains asleep."

He nodded. "Can I have a look at that handbag?"

"Yes." She got it for him.

He took it and carefully removed the contents of the top section on a nearby table. Then he opened the secret bottom and took out the jewels. Holding the diamond necklace in his hand, he gave a jaded glance at the handbag and then at Clare.

"Such an old-fashioned and simple stunt not even the slickest customs officer would be looking for it," he said.

"What do you think?" she asked.

He carefully gathered the many items of jewelry in a large white hankie. "I'll have to make a call," he told her carefully. He went over to the phone and dialed a number. The conversation that ensued was carried on in such a low voice she was unable to make any sense out of it.

At last he ended his talk and hung up. He came back to her with the jewels still bundled in the white handkerchief and with a grim expression on his face.

"I've just made a check," he said.

"Yes?" Her hands were clasped nervously.

"Prepare yourself for a shock," he said.

Her eyes opened wide. "What kind of shock?"

"You have been on the wrong track."

"What do you mean?"

Munson smiled thinly. "These jewels weren't stolen from anyone. They are the property of Miss Faith."

"Oh, no!" she gasped.

"That's right," the Federal man said. "I

just checked the items. So there's nothing to do but put them back in the handbag and forget all about it." He crossed to the table where he'd left the bag.

Clare followed him, completely upset now. "But I was so sure! I mean, Gloria Faith had been under suspicion!"

Munson was busy restoring the handbag to its former state. He gave her a knowing glance. "You did the right thing," he said. "No one will blame you."

"Mr. Benson will!"

"Don't worry about it," the Federal man advised. "You made a normal mistake. And you were perfectly right in bringing the jewels to Mr. Benson's attention."

"I feel so guilty," she said unhappily.

"About her?" the Federal man said. "Don't waste sympathy on her. She may still be behind the smuggling. All this proves is that these are her own jewels."

"She said they were, but I didn't believe her." Clare said.

The Federal man closed the bag. "Think nothing more about it. I'll be on my way. No one has been hurt. I'll probably see you again." He smiled a thin smile. "I hope we have more luck next time."

She let him out and then closed the door, feeling like a perfect idiot. She would do some tall thinking before she jumped to conclusions so quickly again.

She waited as long as she dared before waking Gloria Faith to get ready for the five o'clock flight to Chicago. Again the dark-haired woman proved difficult to rouse. But under Clare's coaxing she took a cold shower and some black coffee. By the time she was dressed in her street clothes again, she was in almost normal condition.

Gloria eyed her across the table with her coffee cup still in hand. "I owe you a lot for picking up the pieces," she said.

Clare smiled. "You can congratulate me when you reach Chicago and step on stage on time."

The dark woman's pale, lined face showed a rueful smile. "I even believe you'll manage that."

"It's going to be close," Clare warned her, "especially if the flight is delayed or slowed down."

"My own fault," the star said. "I was a fool to start drinking on the way over from London. But Ben kept arguing and threatening to walk out as my personal manager if I didn't agree to a tour he'd lined up in South America. I couldn't see it, and so we finished by having a rousing quarrel."

"I know," she said.

Gloria sighed and placed her coffee cup on the table. "Ben wasn't a much better manager than he was a husband. And now he's brought his record up-to-date. He's walked out on me in both capacities."

"Perhaps he'll be on hand when you get to Chicago?" she suggested.

"Not Ben," the dark woman said. "He's counting on my missing that show. Then he'll start trying to fill in my dates with another gal he's been managing. I know how he operates."

The phone rang, and Clare answered it. She told Gloria, "The limousine is waiting to take us back to the terminal. We'll have to go right down."

"I'm in good shape now," Gloria said, rising and picking up her handbag. "Thanks for keeping your eye on this."

"I didn't mind," Clare said hastily, avoiding looking at her. "I was glad to do it."

Chapter Seven

The weather was good and the jet taking them to Chicago was on time. Clare sat with the star in comfortable first class seats.

Clare said, "We should be in around seven-thirty."

"And we've still got to get into the city to the Blackstone Theatre," Gloria said. "Also, it takes me a little time to make up and get ready for the show."

"What about your accompanist?"

"He'll be at the theatre in Chicago," the star said.

"The O'Hare Airport is the busiest one in the country," Clare told the star by way of conversation. "It serves twenty air lines."

"And it must be twenty miles from the center of the city," Gloria said gloomily. "It will depend on traffic how long it takes us to get to the theatre."

Clare could tell the star was on edge. She was only thankful Gloria had not shown any disposition to drink again or take any of the pills that had made her ill earlier in the day.

She asked the star, "Where do you go after this performance?"

"I'm booked for Carnegie Hall on Saturday night," Gloria said with a deep sigh. "But that's a long way off at the moment."

Gloria Faith's tension and moodiness greatly increased as they landed at the Windy City airport. She clutched her handbag nervously and kept urging Clare to lose no time finding them a taxi. They'd just entered the terminal when a young man wearing the uniform of a Trans-Continental porter approached them.

"Miss Andrews?" he inquired politely.

"Yes," she said.

"Mr. Benson asked that I meet you and Miss Faith," he said. "He has arranged for a helicopter to take you into the city."

"Wonderful!" Clare exclaimed, feeling relieved. She turned to the star. "You see, you had no need to worry. A helicopter will get us downtown in no time."

"I hope you're right," Gloria said dubiously.

"Just come with me, ladies," the porter said.

Now Gloria began to be concerned about her luggage. But the porter assured her it would be taken in the helicopter as well. As soon as they boarded the whirlybird, they fastened their seat belts. The craft left at once. They landed gently on the roof of a tall building. In a few minutes they were being helped out and rushed to a stairway which led to an elevator which sped them to street level.

A waiting taxi took them and their bags to the Blackstone Theatre; Gloria still had twenty-five minutes to spare. Strangely, the moment the star walked through the stage door she became assured again. She gave instructions as to where her bags should be taken and called her accompanist-orchestra leader to her dressing room for a consultation as she began to make up.

Clare stood quietly in the background as people came and went. The big dressing room seemed to have become the nerve center of the famous old theatre. A maid helped Gloria Faith change into her first costume of the evening, a gold lamé mini-dress. The star's face had undergone an almost complete transformation through the magic of stage make-up.

Turning to Clare, she smiled. "Do I look like the hag you took under your wing at Kennedy Airport this morning?"

Clare smiled thinly. "You look very well."

The star glanced in the mirror again. "It will do," she said. "Of course it's all fake, just as everything about me is a fake these days, including my voice."

"The public can't think so," Clare told her. "I hear the house is filled."

Gloria Faith sighed. "Yes, they still come, mostly to feed on the memory of what I used to be. I don't think a lot of them notice my voice is gone. They listen and remember what it was formerly, and that's what they hear." She gave Clare a bitter smile. "How lucky for me!"

There was a knock on the dressing room door. "Curtain, Miss Faith," a man's voice said.

"Thank you," Gloria called out in reply. She stood up and turned facing Clare. "Now, my dear, you must go into the audience and see the show, since it is largely due to you there is one tonight."

"No need," Clare demurred. "I can watch from the wings."

"You'd make me nervous," the star said. "I want you to see it from the back of the theatre."

Clare followed her out to the exciting world of backstage. In the shadows, the star sought out the stage manager and had him delegate a man to lead Clare down a flight of steps and along a passage that took them by the lower boxes to a side aisle leading to the rear of the crowded theatre. There were no seats left, so she stood in the back.

She hardly had time to look around before the house lights dimmed and a current of hushed excitement seemed to surge through the crowded theatre. A spotlight focused on the orchestra pit, and the leader appeared and bowed to a round of applause. Then he lifted his baton in the air as a cue to the orchestra to begin a medley of famous Gloria Faith hit tunes; songs she had made famous in the days when she was a young and lovely film star.

The overture ended on a high pitch of emotion, and the curtain was drawn up to reveal a darkened, empty stage with a single white spotlight. Then from the shadows the elfin figure of Gloria Faith appeared, to stand in the shaft of cold light. Her appearance had an instant effect on the audience. Many stood up, others cheered, and there were even a few whistles. It took several minutes and repeated playing of the star's introductory song before the crowd quieted enough for her to begin.

When she did start to sing, a great deal of the magic was lost for Clare. In spite of the excellent orchestra, the fine arrangements and the expert staging and lighting, there was little to remind one of the old Gloria

Faith in the star's grating rendition of her repertoire of hits. And yet it didn't seem to matter to her audience. They applauded each and every number with wild enthusiasm. Gloria responded warmly from the stage, tossing kisses as a token of her appreciation and finally sitting down on the outer edge of the stage, close to the orchestra leader, to sing her best known number. This brought the first half of the show to a conclusion, and there was thunderous applause until the lights came up full.

Clare decided to stay where she was for the balance of the show.

The second half of the program was shorter than the first. Gloria made some quick, spectacular costume changes. A young male dancer appeared to fill in the time when she was off-stage. Then came the final medley of her most popular songs and another demonstration of fanaticism by the audience. Most of them were on their feet applauding and cheering as the curtain finally came down.

Clare was unable to return backstage for some minutes after the show ended, as the aisles were clogged with people on the way out. As soon as an opportunity presented itself, she quickly made her way down the side aisle and retraced her steps backstage to the star's dressing room. A cluster of fans had also found their way to her door.

The stage manager had taken a stand at the door and was telling them, "I'm sorry; Miss Faith is not feeling well enough to see anyone tonight. No autographs tonight. Miss Faith is very tired." He kept up variations of this until most of the star's fans left, although a few stood their ground firmly hoping to pounce on her when she finally emerged. The stage manager saw Clare and, recognizing her, made a motion to her to join him.

The big man smiled as she came near and said, "You can go right in, nurse." He opened the door for her, and she slipped inside. She did not immediately see Gloria, who was in a side dressing room changing. But a moment later the star appeared in a rose dressing gown, holding a tall glass partly filled with amber liquid.

Clare realized she reacted visibly to this, for the star suddenly burst into a harsh laugh. "Don't look so shocked," Gloria Faith said. "I always unwind with some bourbon after a performance."

"It's just that you've had such a difficult day," Clare said awkwardly.

The star smiled at her knowingly. "Your responsibility is over now."

"Not really," Clare said. "I won't feel that way until you're safely back in New York."

Gloria helped herself to a generous mouthful of the bourbon and then sat down by her dressing room mirror, facing Clare. The star's face wore an amused expression. "You seem to have adopted me," she said.

"I'm only following my orders."

"Why should Trans-Continental take such an interest in me? No air line ever has before."

"You've been a very good customer of ours," Clare pointed out.

The star took another drink of the amber liquid, then said, "Very well. Wait until I'm dressed, and we'll go back to the hotel together. I hope you liked the show."

"I don't know where you found the energy for the long performance," Clare said. "The audience loved you."

Gloria's ravaged face was derisive. "And what about you? Were you enchanted by my variation of a whiskey voice?"

Clare was embarrassed by the star's frankness. "I think you did very well."

"I know," Gloria Faith said with a sigh. "Very well for someone who hasn't any voice left at all. Sit down. I won't be long dressing."

Clare said little else as Gloria kept up a

conversation with the maid, mostly about show business personalities they both knew. She did note that the star refilled her glass when it was empty, but there was little she could do about that except feel badly for her. At last Gloria was in her street clothes, and they took a taxi to the luxury hotel in which the star always stayed when in the Windy City.

Early the following morning they took a return flight to New York. To Clare's dismay, the star began ordering drinks almost as soon as they were in the air. Although she kept a drink in front of her during the entire flight, she showed scant signs of drunkenness. Yet the damage to her general health, appearance and talent was all too evident.

"You don't want to join me?" Gloria asked, holding up a martini.

"No thanks."

"Wise girl," Gloria said, then took a sip of her cocktail. "This stuff is poison. But it's too late for me to do anything about it, too late for me to do anything about anything."

Clare felt instant sympathy for the haggard woman at her side. "I think you're wrong about that."

The star smiled wearily. "Don't try to understand. You couldn't if you wanted to.

You're much too young and filled with romantic notions." She paused to stare out at the islands of cloud formations, with only the drone of the jet to break the silence. After taking another sip of her martini, she turned to Clare again. "I had a phone call from Ben this morning."

"Oh?"

"He wants me to take him back," the star said. "Not as a husband, of course. He just wants to be reinstated as my personal manager. He admitted he made a bad mistake in walking out on me yesterday and asked to be forgiven."

Clare said, "That's good news, isn't it?"

The star smiled grimly. "Hardly," she said. "If I'd missed that show last night, he'd be on the phone now trying to book that new girl of his into all my other dates. But I made it and spoiled his scheme. So now he wants back."

"Knowing all that, will you let him handle your affairs again?"

Gloria sipped her martini. "I will," she said at last in a dull voice. "I have to depend on him. There is no one else. No one at all." And she stared out at the clouds once more.

Clare could not help but realize that this woman who had known so much fame and adulation had experienced little true love.

The bitter facts of her existence had turned her into a neurotic alcoholic and destroyed her looks and talent. The life she was living now was one of desperate flight, a retreat in which her pathetic concert appearances marked stands along the way.

They arrived at Kennedy Airport a little before noon. Clare walked with the star to the taxi stand. They shook hands in parting, and Clare said, "I wish you luck on Saturday night."

"I'll manage in the usual way," the sad-faced woman said with one of her wry smiles. "Thank you for everything."

"It was a glamorous experience for me," Clare said.

Gloria Faith looked bleak. "If you haven't already found out, take my word for it now. Don't rate glamor too highly." With a sigh, she collected herself. "Well, I must hurry. I'm meeting Ben at the Plaza for luncheon. We have a lot of things to settle."

Clare watched until the dark woman was in a taxi. A gloved hand waved to her from the taxi window as the star was driven off to the city. Clare suddenly felt letdown and sad. She had come to like Gloria Faith in their brief association. She wished the star well but was deeply worried about her.

She took the escalator up to the second

level and then went directly to the V.I.P. lounge. There were only a few passengers there, and she was greeted by a tall brown-haired girl in a stewardess uniform whom she'd never met before.

She asked the stranger. "Where is Isobel?"

The brown-haired stewardess said, "Her mother is very ill in the hospital. She had to leave just after she came to work."

Clare nodded. "I remember. She's having an operation."

"They don't expect her to pull through. So they called Isobel to the hospital."

"I'm sorry," she said.

"You're Nurse Andrews, aren't you?"

"Yes. How are you making out?"

The brown-haired girl sighed. "Not too badly. We had a heart case yesterday after-noon. Isobel thought he was having an an-gina attack. We paged a doctor downstairs and one came up. It was a heart attack, and the man was sent to the hospital."

"I'm glad you made out," Clare said.

"Are you coming back to work now?"

"I will as soon as I've had lunch," Clare told her.

"Great," the other girl said. "I don't relish being here alone."

Clare went quickly to her office. First she

tried to get Arnold Benson on the line, but he was in conference. However, the prim secretary recognized her voice.

The secretary said, "Mr. Benson suggested you leave any message with me."

"I see," she said. "Then you can tell him we got back safely this morning. Miss Faith managed very well. Nothing unusual happened."

"I'll let him know," the secretary said. "He can call you if he wants any additional information."

Next Clare called Hester in the business office. "I'm back," she said. "And I'm going to lunch now. Can you join me?"

"I was just about to leave my desk," Hester told her. "I'll meet you at the cafeteria entrance."

Hester was so excited about the trip to Chicago with the star she barely took time to pick up a proper lunch for herself. As soon as they were seated, her apartment mate leaned forward eagerly.

"You must have had a thrilling time. Did you meet a lot of show people?"

Clare smiled thinly. "Gloria's accompanist and the stage manager."

Her friend looked disappointed. "But I thought there would be parties and a lot of stars showing up!"

"It was only an overnight trip," Clare reminded her. "And we had very little time. Gloria was not in good condition. We went straight to the theatre, and afterward we went directly to the hotel. This morning we took the plane home."

Hester stared at her sadly. "Then nothing happened?"

"Not really. I saw the show."

"She's an awful drunk, isn't she?"

Clare gave her friend a reprimanding look. "She's a very unhappy woman."

Hester took the hint. "I know. Professional secrecy. I'm sorry I brought it up."

"What news have you for me?"

"Harry is back."

Clare glanced around the crowded cafeteria. "It's a wonder he isn't here now."

"He may be busy. He only got back last night. He called, and I said you were out of town and I wasn't sure when you'd return. He didn't sound too happy."

She smiled. "I suppose not. I'll probably hear from him later today."

"And your other boy friend phoned. Boyle Heath."

"What did he want?"

"He said to tell you he was going to the West Coast for a few days. He'll be in touch with you when he returns."

123

"Fine," Clare said. "He's probably gone out there to see about a new show."

"Are you serious about that actor?" her friend asked.

"I like him a great deal."

"A lot of people noticed you with him when he came here for lunch," Hester said. "And you had him up in the control tower afterward."

Clare showed amusement. "You're well informed."

"I don't miss much," Hester said. "And the best news of all is that Dick has a new hardtop. It's white with a vinyl roof."

"So his prosperity is continuing," Clare said. "He didn't lose much time buying a car."

"He says he expects to have plenty of extra cash coming in," Hester enthused. "Isn't it wonderful?"

"Don't count on it too much," Clare warned her. "The stock market can be tricky." She was really worrying that Dick might be the pilot mixed up in the smuggling, but she'd not been able to find words to break this unhappy suspicion to her friend.

"I think Dick's friend understands the market well," Hester said. "I'm not afraid."

"I wish you both good luck," Clare said

sincerely. They finished their lunch and both went back to their respective departments.

The new girl in the V.I.P. lounge was waiting for Clare when she returned. "Isobel called in," she announced. "Her mother died just a little while ago."

"I'm so sorry," Clare said at once.

"Isobel said she'd be out at least three or four days."

"She should take the rest of the week," Clare said. "I guess that means you'll have to stay on here with me."

"I don't mind that," the brown-haired girl said, "just as long as I'm not left here alone."

The girl went to have her lunch, and Clare took over the affairs of the V.I.P. lounge for the first time since her trip to Chicago.

The phone call she'd expected from Harry came late in the afternoon. "You're a hard person to catch," he said in a bantering tone.

"I've been waiting to hear from you," she said.

"Let's have dinner together," he suggested.

"All right," she said. "Where?"

"I'd like to make it early," he told her. "A lot of work has piled up since I left. I'm coming back to work tonight. Suppose we meet at the International Motel. They have a pretty good dining room, and it's right here at the airport."

"I feel a fright," she said. "I'd rather go home and find something fresh to wear."

"Okay," he said reluctantly. "You can do that, and we can still meet at the International. Let's make it six-thirty, and I'll do some work before I go over there."

She laughed. "This is a new twist for us: dining at the airport."

"I didn't think you'd find it so odd." Harry's voice sounded full of meaning. "After all, you had lunch with Boyle Heath at the cafeteria the other day."

Clare lost most of her good humor. So Harry knew and was going to make a fuss about it.

Chapter Eight

Harry was waiting for her in the lobby of the International Motel when she arrived a few minutes before six-thirty. She'd gone home and had a bath and changed into a dark green dress and matching topcoat she'd recently bought. Feeling much better, she walked up to the crew cut young executive with a smile.

"I didn't keep you waiting," she said.

"I was beginning to wonder if you would." He gave her a close scrutiny. "You don't show any wear and tear from your trip."

"A bath and a change of clothes did wonders for me," she told him brightly. "And now I feel famished."

"I can recommend the roast beef here," he told her.

Not until after they had ordered did they do much talking. Then Harry studied her across the table with interested eyes as he said, "How did you like being a companion to Gloria Faith?"

"It was an interesting experience."

"Did you find her hard to handle?"

She shook her head. "Not really. In spite of her emotional difficulties, I think she's basically a nice person."

He shrugged. "According to what I heard, she was drunk when she left London and no better when she arrived here."

Clare ignored this. "I did get her to Chicago in time for her show," she said.

"Which, in view of the facts, might be considered a major achievement," Harry said. "But let's forget about Gloria Faith and talk about you. Have you missed me while I was gone?"

"I always do," she said quietly.

"But you did manage to see Boyle Heath."

"I can't see that has anything to do with it."

He bent toward her. "I disagree. According to the story told me, you had him here for lunch and then showed him around the place."

She knew it was something they had to face. "Well?"

"Do you think that was fair to me?"

"I didn't think about you," she said. "He wanted to come out here and see the control tower. It was a chance for us to talk without having an evening date."

Harry's pleasant young face was grim. "I'd hoped you weren't going to see him any more."

"Did I promise you that?"

"No."

"Well then," she said.

He looked unhappy. "Some of the boys have been ribbing me about it."

"You could have told them it wasn't any of their business."

He sighed. "I guess I should have. I don't think you can call me unreasonable, Clare. But there's something about your seeing Boyle Heath that rubs me the wrong way."

Clare smiled. "Wouldn't it be the same with any other man I showed an interest in? You're jealous, terribly so. You may as well admit it."

Harry looked sheepish. "Of course I'm concerned about you."

"Jealous," she underlined firmly. "It's not quite the same thing. You frighten me by your attitude. I'm afraid I could never consider marriage with anyone who wanted to own me so completely."

"Marriage is owning," he said indignantly.

She shook her head. "You see? In my book it's sharing."

"Let's not spend the whole dinner period

playing word games," he said huffily as the waiter came with their food.

Their argument was put aside as they gave their attention to the meal. But Harry was persistent, and again Boyle's name was mentioned over coffee and dessert.

Spooning up his parfait, Harry said, "Everything else apart, Boyle is too old for you."

Clare offered the young man across the table a surprised smile. "He can't be much more than forty."

"That's too old!"

"I find him interesting as a friend," she said. "I wish you'd let it go at that."

The crew-cut young executive said earnestly, "And I wish you'd stop playing around and decide to marry me."

"I have my career to consider."

"Some career!" he scoffed. "Nurse to a lot of spoiled millionaires with indigestion."

"You just can't argue fairly," she told him. "You have to go to extremes. That's not a true statement of my work. And you know it as well as anyone."

"You can go on with your nursing for a while after we're married," Harry said.

"Thank you for your generosity," she said with sarcasm. "It's wonderful to be owned and have one's life all planned out."

"Now don't start that owning business

again," he exclaimed in disgust, and took a big gulp of his coffee.

"Let's just dismiss the subject," she suggested. "There are plenty of other thing to discuss. Have you heard anything else about the smuggling?"

"Nothing new."

"Hester told me that Dick has bought an expensive car, and he seems to think money is going to roll in for him from now on."

Harry poured himself a second cup of coffee from the silver pot left on the table. "Pilots make good salaries," he said.

"But Dick has never known how to manage money. Most of the time he's just lived from pay check to pay check."

"Didn't Hester say something about his having a friend in the stock market?"

She was openly scornful. "That's his story."

"It may be true." Harry put sugar in his coffee and stirred it.

"I don't believe it," was her reply. "I think he's mixed up in some kind of illegal deal. And it could very well be the smuggling."

"I've told you before I don't agree," Harry said with the calmness he always assumed when she brought this up. He went on to ask, "Why are you so anxious to see Dick involved?"

"I don't want to see him involved," she protested. "I'd like to have him cleared. Then I would know it was real prosperity and not worry for Hester's sake."

Harry smiled sourly. "I suppose from your point of view your thinking is logical, but I can't go along with it."

"I'm sorry I brought it up," she said.

He sipped his coffee and teased her by asking, "What other subjects shall we discuss that you think shouldn't be mentioned?"

She sat back ruefully. "Your trip to London didn't improve your disposition."

"And your visit to Chicago didn't put you in a happier frame of mind."

Clare smiled. "Honestly, all we ever do when we're together is argue."

"Which I consider a sound basis for a marriage," he assured her with mock gravity. "We'll settle into the routine without any pain at all."

She laughed gently at this. "Sometimes your jokes are dangerously close to the truth."

"I like to live perilously."

"More and more I see you as the bachelor type," Clare told him.

He touched his napkin to his lips and put it aside. "If I didn't have to go back to work,

I'd spend the evening proving how wrong you are."

She gave him a teasing smile. "And the mere fact you have chosen to go back to work confirms what I've just said. You're the bachelor type."

On this note of friendly taunting they parted.

The following day proved a routine one in the V.I.P. lounge. From the morning papers Clare learned where Isobel's mother was resting and when the funeral would be. She phoned an order for flowers to the funeral home and made up her mind to make a visit to it in the evening. With luck she might catch the blonde girl there.

One of the passengers waiting for the Hawaii flight was a popular night club comedian named Happy Wood. Happy was a diminutive little man with an owl-like face and a very serious manner when he wasn't performing. He also had a great interest in statistics. On top of everything else, he was terribly afraid of traveling by plane.

He cornered Clare and insisted she go out on the promenade with him. It was another warm spring day, and he pointed to the great Boeing jet which he was soon to board with the other passengers and said, "I'm scared witless of getting aboard that thing."

She smiled at him. "Then all those jokes you make in your night club act about being afraid of planes are real?"

"Absolutely on the level," the little man in the sporty gray suit told her solemnly. "I think that's why the routine never fails to get laughs. They know I mean it."

"You should try to get over your phobia," she advised. Glancing back at the lounge, she reminded him, "None of the other passengers is worried. They're all looking forward to the flight."

Happy Wood's owl face showed even more despair. "They haven't got my kind of mind. That's an awful small hunk of steel to be up there in all that air."

Clare saw a chance to make statistics do some work for her. She asked the comedian, "How much do you weigh?"

He stopped gazing at the shining jet with its attendant trucks, fuel tanks and mechanics around it. He said, "I'm a lightweight, Nurse. I'm just a hundred and four pounds."

"That jet weighs three hundred and eleven thousand pounds when it's loaded," she said. "So it's not as small as you think."

"It's pretty big," he agreed.

She quickly followed up with, "And its wing span is more than a hundred and fifty feet. It has four engines with a total horse-power of seventy-two thousand pounds, and it can cruise at a speed of five hundred miles an hour for close to five thousand miles."

"Hey! Wait a minute!" the little man said. "You're drowning me in figures!"

Clare laughed. "I just wanted you to get the facts right. That jet isn't as big as an ocean liner, but it's plenty large enough."

Happy Wood looked doleful. "Even when you prove it, I don't want to believe it."

"You're just afraid if you lose your fear of planes, your night club act will be a flop," she accused him.

"You could be right," the comedian admitted. And he gave her no more trouble.

The day passed uneventfully, and as Hester had already left for dinner with Dick, Clare made a simple evening meal for herself at the apartment. After she'd cleaned up the dishes, she changed her clothes and took the bus to the funeral parlor, whose address she had written down.

When she arrived there Isobel, looking pale and wearing a black knit dress, was bidding goodbye to an elderly couple who were neighbors and had come to pay their final respects. Clare waited until they left and then joined the blonde girl.

135

"Thanks for the flowers," Isobel said. "It is so good of you to come way out here."

"I wanted to come," she said.

They stood in the cool, shadowy surroundings of the austere funeral parlor. It was decorated in gray, and the simple casket in the corner was under the glow of a floor lamp to the left of it. There was a sparse number of floral tributes and an open visitors' book on a stand.

Isobel said, "Please sign the book."

"Of course," Clare said. And she did so. They hesitated awkwardly a moment.

Then Isobel said, "At least Mother didn't suffer much in the end."

"I'm glad," Clare said. "And you must be, too. She was sick such a long time." She moved across to the casket and stood for a moment staring at the thin, strong face that even now still showed a hint of Isobel's fragile beauty. Then they moved away to sit on a divan that was the only large piece of furniture in the room.

"I'll be lonely," Isobel said.

Clare nodded. "But you'll also be able to plan your future as you like. It means you can go back to flying again."

The blonde girl smiled faintly. "I've been wanting to do that. But now I'm free, it doesn't seem important."

"But it will, after the initial shock is over."

The other girl nodded. "I'm sure it would be best for me to get away. I can find another apartment and share it with girls working with me."

"That's what you did before."

"It's the best arrangement," Isobel said. "And of course the company looked after our lodgings and meals in other cities."

They talked a while longer, and then Clare left. She felt sorry for Isobel but knew that what had happened would be best for the blonde girl in the long run. She had been faithful in her duty to her mother, and now that duty was at an end. Isobel could return to the flying she loved.

When the flight from London disembarked the following morning, one of the first people to present himself in the V.I.P lounge was the playboy, René Le Blanc. So many things had happened since she'd talked with him Clare had almost forgotten all about the charming young Frenchman.

He stood before her in natty sport clothes and a white turtle-neck sweater. "Well, Miss Andrews," he said, "I am back at last."

"So you are," she replied.

"And when are we going to have our little chat?" René asked suavely.

"I don't know," she said, wondering how

to handle the situation. Arnold Benson had given her strict orders to encourage him. But she was reluctant to do so, since she had enough romantic problems with Harry and Boyle.

As she hesitated, he asked, "When do you have a day off?"

"Tomorrow is my free afternoon," she said. "But we have one girl out. I'm not sure if I'll get it this week."

"When will you know?" the handsome young Frenchman asked.

"By the morning," she ventured. At least this would give her time to speak to Arnold Benson and see if his instructions were still the same.

"I'll call you here in the morning," René Le Blanc promised. "I am most anxious to present my proposition to you."

"All right," she said weakly. He had an overpowering manner that demanded acquiescence.

The young man nodded brightly and stalked off, leaving her to contend with the usual quota of problems among the V.I.P. passengers. As soon as the rush was over and the next flight had left, she put a call through to Arnold Benson's office. This time she was fortunate in getting the austere head of Trans-Continental at once. As soon as he heard her voice, he said, "I have been intending to call you, Miss Andrews, and congratulate you on the excellent manner in which you took care of that Gloria Faith business."

"I'm calling about someone else," she said. "René Le Blanc left here a short time ago. And he wants to see me tomorrow afternoon."

"Then by all means see him," Arnold Benson said. "We want all the information we can get on that young man."

"We'll be short a girl here if I take my usual afternoon off," she reminded him.

"That presents no problem," he said. "Let me take care of it."

It was later in the afternoon that the Federal man, Munson, presented himself in the V.I.P. lounge. The square-faced, gray-haired man was his usual self-effacing self. Clare took him directly to her office.

When they were alone, he fixed her with a shrewd stare and said, "Mr. Benson told me about your call to him."

"Yes," she said uncertainly.

The middle-aged man in the dark suit frowned. "I'm not sure I'm in agreement with the way the air line is trying to cope with this crisis. It means putting amateurs like yourself up against professional criminals. I would be happier if the entire investigation was left to us." He sighed. "But Mr. Benson has his own theories."

"I understand," she said quietly.

"We've just about eliminated Gloria Faith as a suspect," Munson went on. "But we've strong suspicions concerning René Le Blanc."

"So I understand," Clare said.

"Then there's the financier, Fritz Manner. He may be the money man behind the entire operation. But you won't have seen him lately. He's been living in the South of France."

"He hasn't been in the lounge for some time," she agreed.

The Federal man's strong jaw was set grimly. "If the noose tightens, he'll be showing up. There are members of the Trans-Continental staff we think are mixed up in this. If we can get one of them to talk, we'll soon round up the rest."

With her mind on Dick and his sudden affluence, she asked, "There is a pilot involved, isn't there?"

He gave her a sharp glance. "How do you know that?"

Flustered, she said, "Someone told me."

"Who?"

"I can't remember for the moment."

The Federal man looked as if he didn't believe her. He said dryly, "When you do remember, I wish you'd tell me."

"I will," she said.

"You're to meet this Le Blanc tomorrow."

"He said he'd call."

"Here's my number," Munson said, offering her a card. "As soon as he calls and you've arranged where you're to meet, let me know."

She took the card and glanced at the number written on it. "If he doesn't call?" she wanted to know.

"Better phone me anyway. If I'm not there, say who it is, and I'll call you back. Understand?"

"Yes."

The Federal man turned to go and then added, "Once we know where you're meet- ing him, we'll have someone there. We'll keep you covered all the time. As I say, we're worried about exposing amateurs like yourself to possible danger. So we'll try to cut the risk down as much as possible."

"Thank you," she said. "I hope it is soon cleared up."

"We all do," Munson said. "So far we've been able to keep it out of the papers. Once the story breaks, the gang is liable to break up and go under cover and we'll never get them."

"I see," she said, still holding his card.

He hesitated. "One more thing, Miss Andrews."

"Yes?" She waited tensely for what he would say next.

The Federal man looked uncomfortable. "It's about my mother-in-law. She has arthritis bad. Are aspirins the best remedy for that kind of pain?"

It was a letdown for her. She almost laughed at his question. But she could see he had put it to her in all seriousness. "Yes," she said. "It seems to be generally agreed that aspirin is excellent for arthritis pains."

"She takes a lot of them."

"I doubt if they'll do her any harm," Clare assured him.

"Thanks," the Federal man said. "I've been worried. And don't forget to call me as soon as you hear from that playboy."

He left her in a tense state. In fact, she got little sleep that night. And in the morning she was so edgy even Hester noticed it and suggested she needed a holiday. She'd been on duty in the lounge only for about an hour when the expected phone call came.

"Will you be free this afternoon?" René Le Blanc asked eagerly.

"Yes, I will be," she said.

"Excellent," the jet set favorite told her. "This could mean a lot of money for you. We'll meet at the Central Park entrance to the Plaza and have tea in the Palm Court."

"What time?" she asked in a small voice, once again feeling like a female Judas.

"Let us make it four-thirty," the young Frenchman said.

As soon as the conversation ended, she placed the call to the Federal man. Munson answered the phone himself and heard her story. "The Palm Court of the Plaza at four-thirty," he said. "We'll look after it. And that bit about your making a lot of money through him is really funny. We've checked and found out Le Blanc has been borrowing wildly from a lot of his old friends. He's been in a money bind ever since his last wife divorced him and cut him off her payroll."

Chapter Nine

Clare found herself terribly nervous as the time approached for her meeting with playboy René Le Blanc. She had dressed carefully in a gray tweed suit that was a favorite with her and wore a neat black velvet hat styled in the fashion of a London bobby's helmet. It was a chic outfit, and she felt it would be right for the fashionable Plaza Hotel.

Having arrived in the city early for the appointment, she did some window shopping along Fifth Avenue. It was a lovely day, not too warm for the season, but bright with sunshine. She stopped by Peck & Peck's smart women's shop near the Plaza and made a quick inspection of some new fashions. She saw several items that interested her but had no time to try them on, so she left, making a mental note to come by again at her first opportunity.

She now had only a few minutes to spare, so she crossed Fifth Avenue and hurried up to the Central Park entrance of the majestic old hotel as René Le Blanc had instructed her. She was becoming increasingly nervous, and she wondered where the Federal man watching her would be and if she would recognize him. Mounting the granite steps of the entrance, she entered the lobby and looked around for René Le Blanc.

He was nowhere in sight, so she stood in the crimson-carpeted lobby with its high ornate ceilings and decor of another era. The place was busy with people bustling in all directions as usual. Then a smiling René came striding down past the desk area with a hand outstretched. He looked unusually handsome in a dark suit, white shirt and discreet black tie. Reaching her, he took her hand in his and drew her close for an affectionate kiss on the cheek.

"Forgive me for keeping you waiting," he said. "A phone call came just as I was ready to come out here to meet you."

She smiled up into his tanned face. "I've only been here a moment."

Lightly guiding her by the arm, he said, "Come along. I have our table reserved."

Clare walked with him along the broad corridors leading to the famed Palm Court, a fenced-in palm-decorated restaurant area located in the middle of the vast lobby. A headwaiter greeted René by name at the entrance to the exclusive spot and led them to a suitably remote white-clothed table. The place was already well-filled, and in the rear a pianist played popular selections as a strolling violinist wandered between the tables. It was New York's most fashionable rendezvous for afternoon tea or cocktails and also for light after-theatre snacks.

Clare drew off her black leather gloves and smiled across the table at René Le Blanc. "This is very nice," she said.

"The sandwiches and French pastries are excellent," he assured her.

A waiter came and took their order. Clare chose tea along with a selection of sandwiches and pastries. René asked for coffee and the same. Some of her uneasiness had left her in the relaxing surroundings, but she still was well aware of what the meeting might mean to her.

"I worried that you might not come," the handsome playboy said.

"I said I would," she reminded him. "I usually keep my word."

He lifted a hand in a gesture of resignation. "Too often I have found attractive women lacking in this respect," he said. "My last wife was almost always late for appointments or never kept them at all."

She offered him a slight smile. "I keep forgetting. You have recently been divorced again."

He nodded. "I have not had much luck in my marriages." His face brightened. "Yet I have not lost faith in the institution."

"All your wives have been enormously wealthy," she reminded him. "I think that sometimes makes for difficult temperaments."

The playboy shrugged. "I cannot say with any certainty. In Europe it is so different. I find many American customs difficult to understand."

She might have been amused by this under other circumstances. Surely René had found it convenient to wed a series of young American girls with comfortable fortunes. It was well known that he'd been a photographer for a minor Paris magazine before his wives' money had enabled him to cut a wide swath in the café society of the Old and New Worlds.

The waiter came with their orders. And at the same time a lone male was shown to a table adjacent to them. Clare had a hard time stifling any obvious reaction to this new arrival. For the man who was now sitting almost within earshot of them was Munson. The Federal man was wearing a subdued gray suit and looked like any of the wealthy businessmen in the room. He paid no attention to their table at all but concentrated on the menu. Yet she had no doubt that he would keep a close check on them.

Over the sandwiches, Rene said, "I suppose you have been wondering why I invited you here?"

"I have," she said frankly.

He smiled, showing excessively white teeth against his bronzed skin. "You have been trying to guess what the mystery is? How I am able to offer you a chance to make a great deal of money?"

"Wouldn't you consider that natural?" she said, studying him closely. "My present position offers limited earnings."

"And no opportunity for advancement with the air line," Rene Le Blanc pointed out. "No matter what, you will always be only a nurse."

"Yes," she said. "I've thought of that."

"In this world, money is the important thing," the playboy assured her. "You have only to look around this restaurant to realize that. I can fix it so you will earn some real cash."

"You're making me more curious every moment," she said with a smile. She could see by the way Munson was sitting at the other table that he was listening to everything they said. It gave her some badly needed assurance and poise to know this.

The jet set favorite took a sip of his coffee, and, with the cup still in hand, said, "You perhaps have been thinking I have been offering you some kind of fantastic story, what you would call a line. Is that not so?"

She nodded. "It has occurred to me."

"You could not be more wrong," he said, putting the cup down. He paused. "You probably know that I am not a rich man."

"I think the papers have mentioned it."

He smiled wryly. "Nothing is personal or sacred in the press today. The journalists take pleasure in pointing out that I have invariably married for money." He paused to shrug. "If so, I would say that I have offered excellent value. I have always been an attentive and understanding husband. But now that is at an end. My record of failure has been complete."

"So?"

"So I am embarking on a new project," René Le Blanc said, "one in which you can be of great assistance."

Clare's nervous tension had reached a high point. A glance showed her that the Federal man was drinking in every word of their talk. Bracing herself for the revelation that must come momentarily, she asked, "Isn't it time you shed the mystery and told me what you have in mind?"

René Le Blanc laughed lightly. "You American women are so direct."

"It's not such a bad quality."

"But difficult for one like myself to comprehend," the playboy said. "Still, I agree that now is the moment for me to offer you the facts."

"I'm listening," she said.

"You may feel there is some risk on your part," he said carefully, "that what I suggest might change your way of life."

"Oh?"

"But I feel the rewards are rich enough to compensate for the problems involved."

She could sense his hesitancy in arriving at the heart of the matter. And his reluctance to come out frankly with what he had in mind increased her suspicion that he was about to ask her to help in some way with the gem smuggling.

Munson was bent over his plate now, but she felt certain the Federal man was still listening to them. She said, "I accept the assurance that the work you have in mind offers good money. What about the details?"

René hesitated a moment longer. Then he

said, "I must swear you to secrecy in this matter. It would be disastrous for me if any of what I'm about to tell you should reach other ears."

"I understand," she said.

"I must have your promise of silence whether you come in with me or not," he insisted.

"I'll agree to that," she said.

"Very well," René said. "I have been raising funds from a number of my friends, and I'm about to launch a photographic and advertising agency in this country. You know that I was once a photographer?"

"Yes, I do," she said, somewhat confused.

"I'm confident I can operate a very successful advertising firm," he went on. "I have prominent social names willing to offer testimonials for certain products; people an ordinary advertising firm could not approach but who will cooperate with me because I have their friendship. And I have the idea of using attractive girls in various lines of work to pose for advertisements pertaining to their special careers. In other words, my models will be professionals in the fields they pose for. As a nurse, you would be featured in medical advertisements, toiletries and the like. I already have the manufacturer of a first-aid kit ready to use you as a model for a magazine and television series of advertisements."

The revelation was so completely unexpected that Clare found herself at a loss for words for a moment. She glanced across at the Federal man, but he sat relaxed in his chair as if not at all upset by what he had heard.

She said, "You're asking me to join your agency as a model?"

"That's the idea," he said. "You're certainly pretty enough."

Clare forced a smile. "Thanks. But it's something that has never interested me. I don't think I'd like that kind of life."

"The pay is big."

"I know," she agreed. "But I am a nurse. That is what I trained to be. With the current scarcity of trained nurses, I don't feel like deserting my profession. I sometimes even feel a little guilty about my present job, although I'll surely return to hospital nursing again at some future time."

The handsome playboy looked disappointed. "Then I take it you are refusing my offer."

"I'm afraid I'll have to."

"You would not have to give up your present work," he insisted. "I can arrange for you to come to the agency in the evenings or on your day off."

She hesitated to give him an answer. "I'll have to think about it," she said.

He looked happier. "Then you may work on a part-time basis, after all."

"I'll see," she said. "And as long as I'm employed by Trans-Continental, I have to consider what the company feels about my posing for commercials. If you wanted me to pose in my air line uniform, they might veto the idea."

René frowned. "I don't see why."

"It could be construed as the air line itself endorsing a product," she said.

"We could block out the name on your uniform so it might be any air line," was his suggestion.

"I'll mention it," she said, "and let you know later."

The balance of the tea was an anticlimax as far as Clare was concerned. She finished as quickly as she could and told the handsome playboy that she was meeting a friend. He seemed rather vague and preoccupied, and she guessed that he had expected her to jump at his offer rather than turn it down. When they were ready to leave, the Federal man, Munson, was still seated alone at his table. He was reading a pocket novel as they passed him on the way out and gave no sign of noticing them.

René insisted on accompanying her to the steps. "I will be hearing from you," he said with a pleading look.

"I promise to let you know," she said. "It may take a few days."

After she left the hotel, she hurried to the nearest subway. The time had worked out so that she boarded it at the rush hour. It was a harsh contrast to the soft music and genteel atmosphere of the Palm Court, but she survived the ordeal of the rather long ride back to her apartment area.

When she got there, Hester was already home. The redhead was feeling sorry for herself, as Dick had left on another overseas flight. "We were having so much fun with the new car," she said.

Clare slipped off her hat and jacket. "He'll be back the first of the week," she said with a smile. "It isn't as if he were going to be gone forever." Hester sat on the arm of an easy chair, a frown marring her pretty face. "But he's away so much! It's not so bad when I have you here for company. But after Dick and I are married, I'll be all alone when he's on overseas duty."

"Have you set a date?" Clare asked.

Hester shook her head. "Not yet. But it

will be sooner than we planned. Dick has almost enough money put aside for the down payment on our house."

"And he's bought a new car as well," Clare said. "He's really enjoying prosperity."

"I'm worried," Hester confessed.

"You are?" Clare queried sharply, wondering if the other girl had at last begun to have the same suspicions as she had concerning Dick.

Hester looked mildly surprised. "Yes. I'm afraid his luck in the stock market won't last. It doesn't seem reasonable that it should."

Clare saw she had been mistaken. Hester still was ready to accept the stock market story. She said, "Let's hope he will continue to be lucky awhile longer."

"I do," Hester said fervently.

Clare decided to spend the evening at home. A few minutes before nine the phone rang, and it was for her. When she took the phone she heard Boyle Heath's pleasant, resonant actor's voice over the line.

"I've just gotten back from the West Coast," he said. "I'd like to see you."

"I planned to stay home tonight," she told him.

"Change your plans," he begged. "I've been lonesome for you."

She laughed gently. "I won't listen to that,

not when I know you were out there with all those Hollywood lovelies."

"I didn't see anyone lovelier than you," he said. "And anyway, I didn't have time for girls. I was out there strictly on a business deal. I'll tell you about it when I meet you."

"Some other night, Boyle."

"I'll be at the door of your apartment in a taxi in half an hour," the actor told her. "I'll ring twice and wait for you to come downstairs."

"But I told you!" she protested.

Boyle chuckled. "I wasn't listening," he said, and hung up.

She came back to Hester with the news. "It was Boyle. I told him I didn't want to see him tonight, but he wouldn't take no for an answer. He's coming for me in a taxi. I suppose I'll have to dress."

Hester angrily snapped off the television. "I think that actor has a nerve!" she exclaimed.

"I agree." Clare smiled ruefully. "But what can I do?"

Her girl friend was on her feet now. "I tell you what I'd do," she said firmly. "I'd let him know I had a mind of my own. And I'd break with him altogether."

"But he has a lot of good qualities!"

Hester looked skeptical. "None that his former wives found out," she said. "And you know Harry is jealous. He won't put up with much more."

This annoyed Clare. She started for her own room, saying over her shoulder, "Harry doesn't own me!"

"No. But he has a prior claim!" Hester said, following her.

Clare paused in the doorway. "I think Boyle needs me more than Harry does."

"Now there's a wacky statement if I ever heard one," Hester moaned. "That actor has you hypnotized."

Clare didn't pause to argue any longer. She hurriedly dressed and had no more than gotten ready when the doorbell rang. Hester was sitting disconsolately in the living room as Clare made her way to the door.

Clare smiled at her. "I'll get home early."

"I give up," Hester said. "You just don't want advice."

In a way it was true. At the moment Clare found herself too mixed up to be able to settle anything in her own mind. Advice from others, however well meant, only served further to confuse her. She reached the lower hallway to find Boyle Heath waiting for her.

He smiled and kissed her. "I've been waiting for this moment," he said as they started out to the taxi.

Boyle insisted they return to the city, and

an hour later they were seated in the shadowy atmosphere of the New York Hilton's Italian Room, with its colorful murals of Roman scenes and the lilting music of an all girl trio.

The maturely handsome Boyle smiled at her across the table. "Isn't this better than sitting home?"

"Of course I'm glad to see you," she said. "But I do get tired occasionally. I was in the city all afternoon. I had the offer of a modeling job."

Boyle's eyebrows raised. "From whom?"

She told him, and Boyle Heath listened without making any comment.

She finished by saying, "Of course I'm going to refuse him."

"I'm glad," the actor said. "I don't think you'd like it."

Clare smiled. "It's the sort of thing you've done."

"I've been a male model when there was no other work," he admitted frankly. "A good many actors do fill in between engagements that way. But you are a nurse. You should stick to it."

"I intend to."

"Until you marry," he went on smoothly. "And I have some plans about that. Incidentally, the word from the West Coast is good. I think I have an excellent chance for a new television series."

"I'm so glad," she said sincerely. "When will you know?"

"There are some details to be settled," Boyle said casually. "It may take a few weeks. In the meantime, I'm leaving for London again tomorrow."

"So soon again?"

"Yes," he said. "That's why I wanted to see you tonight. And now let's have a dance or two."

The music was good, and they enjoyed dancing. But Clare noticed that the actor occasionally had trouble with his ailing left leg. She had not been so aware of it in the past. When they returned to their table, she mentioned it tactfully.

"You needn't dance any more if your knee is bothering you," she told him.

Boyle looked guilty. "What makes you think I'm having trouble with it?"

She smiled. "I could tell on the floor. You seemed to drag your leg every once in a while."

The actor sighed. "I'm sorry. You're right. It has been giving me some trouble. It has spells."

"Shouldn't you see a doctor in case it might get worse?"

"No need. It's just a tricky knee. The doctor told me I'd always have recurrent bouts of trouble with it. You learn to live with such things."

Clare had a clinical interest in his problem. "You said it happened in Switzerland?"

"Yes," he replied shortly, and it struck her he was not anxious to discuss it. He confirmed this with his next words. "I don't mention it to most people. The picture of an actor, especially a leading man like myself, with a game knee isn't flattering."

"I understand." She smiled. "I'll forget all about it. But perhaps you should rest it for the balance of the evening."

And they did. Then Boyle saw her home in a taxi. It had been a good evening, and she told him so as he left the taxi waiting to come inside and say good night to her.

She said, "I'll see you at the lounge tomorrow before you go."

Boyle nodded. "Yes. I'm leaving on the noon flight." He paused. "And when I come back I want you to accept my ring. I still have it for you."

"We can discuss that when you come back," she said evasively.

"I won't be put off much longer," he warned her. "I need you. This is a critical time in my life and career." And he took her in his arms for a long kiss.

She smiled up at the actor as he released her. "Am I really all that important to you?"

Boyle Heath's handsome face was deadly serious. "You're the most important person in my life," he said.

She walked upstairs alive with a new happiness. Boyle's love for her and his admitted need of her in his life offered her the fulfillment that every girl sought. While it was true that she'd long thought herself in love with Harry, his increasing coldness and arrogance had turned her from him and made her realize she'd almost made a serious mistake. When Boyle returned from London she'd accept his diamond. Meanwhile, she wouldn't say anything to Hester.

The V.I.P. lounge was busy again the following morning. A driving rain made the day miserable but did not interfere with the movement of air traffic as drizzle and heavy fog would have. Clare was happy to have Isobel back on the job again.

"I felt I would be better here and working," Isobel said simply.

"I agree," Clare said. She took the first opportunity available to phone Arnold Benson. When the general manager of Trans-Continental came on the line, she explained to him about her meeting with René Le Blanc.

"I've already had a report from Munson regarding that," the austere manager of the air line told her. "You handled a difficult situation very well. And by the way, Munson is on his way up to see you now."

She had barely put down the phone and gone out to the main lounge when the Federal man arrived. He was wearing a dark raincoat and battered felt hat and appeared to be in a grim humor.

"Can you spare me a minute?" he asked.

"Come into the office," she said, leading the way.

When they were alone together, he gave her a strange look. "We didn't make out so well with Le Blanc, did we?"

"No. But I was thankful to have you so near. It gave me confidence."

"I'm glad." The Federal's man square faced showed sober satisfaction. Then he asked, "Have you seen the late edition of the morning papers?"

She shook her head. "No."

"Then this will interest you," he said. He drew a folded newspaper out of his jacket pocket and held it out so she could see the headlines. In blaring type was the shocking message: "Trans-Continental Pilot Suicide!"

Chapter Ten

Evidently the Federal man had noticed her stunned reaction to the headline, for in a questioning tone he said, "You seem very upset about this man's suicide."

She looked at the stern, square face. "It is shocking," she murmured.

His eyes narrowed. "Did you know Burt Crandall?"

"Burt Crandall?" she echoed in surprise.

"Yes. That's the pilot who took his life," Munson went on briskly.

Relief surged through her. She shook her head slowly. "No," she said. "I didn't know him."

"I wondered," the Federal man said, sounding as if he weren't quite convinced. "Why did the story bother you so?"

She didn't want to bring up Dick's name in case he might in some way be involved. Improvising quickly, she hurried to say, "I don't quite know. Perhaps because it seemed so needless that a man should sacrifice his life that way."

"Crandall was the pilot we've been watching," Munson told her. "He was one of the key men in the smuggling ring. We were ready to close in on him and hoped through him to get the evidence we needed against the others. He must have had some warning. So he did this." He took the newspaper and folded it, then returned it to his jacket pocket. "And we're left in a worse fix than ever."

She asked, "You have no other definite leads?"

"There is one man on the staff who could be in on the smuggling," Munson said. "But we can't bother him yet."

"What happens next?" Clare asked.

"This suicide may stir things up some," the Federal man said hopefully. "It's my guess that Fritz Manner will be coming back from Europe any day. If he shows up here, keep an eye on him. We're interested in everything about him: whom he has meet him, any phone calls he makes, any remarks he makes to you. A slip of the tongue has put more than one crook behind bars."

"I'll remember," she promised. "Not that I've had much luck with either Gloria Faith or René Le Blanc."

"Le Blanc is in the clear," the Federal man said. "I'm still not sure about the Faith woman. Let me know if she attempts to get in touch with you."

"I will," Clare promised.

The Federal man left, and she returned to her work.

She was just beginning to achieve a feeling of normalcy when an unexpected emergency arose to challenge her again. Isobel was the one who first notified her of the accident. The blonde girl came hurrying over to her.

"A passenger just stumbled on the escalator and cut his hand badly," she said.

"Where is he?" Clare asked.

"He'll be here in a minute," the other girl said. "He's stopped to wrap a handkerchief around it."

Clare waited no longer but rushed out the double doors to meet the accident victim. She spotted him at once; a small, nervous-looking woman was standing at his side. She recognized them from having seen them in the lounge before. It was Paul Rocca, the violinist, and his wife Nella.

Going up to him, she asked, "Did you get a bad cut, Mr. Rocca?"

The tall, dark Rocca glanced at her with piercing eyes under heavy black brows. "Bad enough," he said in his deep voice. "Fortunately, it is my right hand."

Clare knew at once what he meant. Rocca was one of America's most noted concert violinists. And it was the left hand that did all the intricate string work, while the right hand for the most part only manipulated the bow.

"It is still a serious threat," his wife Nella said in her shrill, nervous fashion. "My husband should take action against your company."

"Nella, please!" the tall man reprimanded his wife. "The fault was my own. The soles of my shoes were wet and slippery from the rain. That is why I slipped on the metal stairs. You can't blame Trans-Continental for that."

"You are making a mistake!" his wife warned him. "And what are we going to do about the concert in Detroit tonight?"

"I'll manage," the violinist told her. Giving his attention to Clare, he said, "Enough of such nonsensical talk. Will you see what you can do about this, young lady?" The handkerchief that covered the back of his right hand was already stained red.

"If you'll come into my office," Clare said. "It's off the lounge."

"You should have a doctor at once," the diminutive wife of the violinist insisted shrilly. "Your hands are your fortune."

He gave her a reproving glance. "Please

try to control yourself, Nella. You will wait for me in the lounge while the nurse looks after my injury."

The tiny woman glared at him and then at Clare. But when they entered the lounge she stepped back and allowed Clare to take her husband into the office while she remained outside.

As soon as they were alone, Paul Rocca apologized for his wife. "She means well. But she has a strange protective urge where I'm concerned. She generally overdoes her solicitude."

"I understand," she said. She had previously had a sample of Nella Rocca's difficult disposition. The little woman had raged once before when their flight was delayed in its departure by fog.

She carefully removed the blood-soaked handkerchief from the musician's hand and saw there was a long cut across the back of it. The cut was still welling blood and looked ugly.

She began to clean the wound area. "Are you to play tonight?" she asked.

"Yes," the violinist said. "Our plane is due to leave within a half-hour."

Clare was busy with the wound. She reached for an antiseptic. "This may hurt," she warned him.

"Don't worry about that," he said in a tight voice.

She applied the stinging liquid, and he gave no sign of flinching. Then she carefully bandaged and taped the wound. As she worked, she said, "There's no time to get a doctor here now. But the flight to Detroit won't take long, and you can check with a medical man there."

"You think it is that bad?" he asked.

"I don't know." She sighed. "In an ordinary case I'd regard it as a superficial wound. But you can't be too careful. As your wife said, your hands are your fortune."

He moved his bandaged hand. "It feels better already."

Clare smiled at him. "You are a good patient. But that hand is bound to be stiff and sore." She paused. "It may even need a stitch or two."

"Wouldn't stitches make it more difficult to use?"

"I don't think anyone would recommend you use that hand too vigorously for twenty-four hours at least."

The tall man frowned. "But I have this concert. I shall manage."

"Perhaps you can make out," she agreed. "But it will mean pain and perhaps slower healing."

"I'll take the risk," he said with a smile. "Thank you for your good work, nurse."

"Don't forget to check with a doctor when you reach Detroit," she warned him.

When they went out to rejoin his wife, the little woman eyed his bandaged hand angrily and said, "Well, I see it's been botched up."

"No need to talk that way, Nella," her husband told her. "The nurse has done an excellent temporary job. And I'll have a doctor look at it in Detroit."

"I should hope so." The little woman bridled. And with a malevolent glance for Clare, she warned, "The company hasn't heard the last of this. My husband's lawyers will contact them."

Paul Rocca, who was standing behind his wife, gave Clare a private wink not to take the threat too seriously. So she merely nodded and moved away. A few minutes later the boarding notice for the Detroit flight came over the speakers, and they left.

As soon as the violinist and his wife had gone from the lounge, Isobel came over to her. The blonde girl shook her head. "Wasn't she awful?"

Clare smiled. "She has a low boiling point. And I think the accident did scare her."

"Will he be able to play tonight?"

"I'm sure he will play," Clare told her. "I'm also sure it will be a difficult and painful evening for him."

Now the passengers began to arrive for the London flight. And among them was Boyle Heath. He appeared about forty minutes before the big jet was due to pull out in the rain. He wore no hat but did have on his blue trench coat. His hair was soaked, and rivulets of rain streaked his face as he came up to her.

"Left my brief case behind in the cab," he told her. "Had to chase after it in the rain. But I managed to catch him before he got away."

"It is an awful day," she agreed.

"I wondered if there'd be any delay in departure," he said.

"We've had no word of any. You'll probably fly above the storm."

"Comforting thought," he said with a weary smile. And then, his eyes fixed on hers, he said quietly, "Last night was good."

"I know," she agreed in a soft tone.

"I hate leaving right now."

"It's your career," she said.

"That's so." He sighed. "I'd hate to tell you how many times it has interfered with my private life."

She smiled sympathetically. "It needn't this time."

"You'll be waiting for me?"

"I promise."

The handsome actor glanced around unhappily at the sizable crowd gathered in the lounge. "Isn't there some place we can be alone for a few minutes."

She shook her head. "I'm on duty."

"And I'm a customer of the line. Aren't my wishes important? Isn't it your duty to cater to me?" he asked with mock sternness.

Clare laughed gently. "We'll have lots of time together when you return."

"Like all our lives?"

She arched an eyebrow. "It sounds interesting. And now I will have to leave you for a few minutes. I must check with some of the other passengers."

"My usual fate," he lamented. "I always have to share you with someone."

She left him standing dejectedly near the promenade exit. A few minutes later the boarding notice for the London flight came over the speakers. The crowd began to file out to the down escalator. Boyle lingered to the last.

"I'll get back as soon as I can," he said.

"When do you think that will be?" she asked.

"Probably a week or so," he told her. "It's hard to be sure." And then he caught her by surprise and took her in his arms for a short but satisfactory kiss. He let her go with a smile. "Don't remind me about the company rules against that. I don't happen to work for the company." And he was on his way.

A surprised Isobel came to stand with her and watch after him. The blonde girl said, "I guess you two must be very good friends."

Clare smiled at her. "He could be the man I'm going to marry."

Dick had returned from overseas, and that evening he was at the apartment when Clare arrived after work. Hester poked her head out of the kitchen and said, "I thought we'd eat in because of the rain."

Clare took off her coat. "Sounds like a good idea," she said.

Dick was stretched out on the divan with a magazine. He gave her a friendly smile. "It's good to be back," he said.

She was relieved to be able to talk to him with out worrying that he was mixed up in the smuggling. She asked, "Did you know that Burt Crandall who killed himself?"

Dick sat up with a grim expression. "Sure. He was a nice guy. I never guessed he'd do a thing like that."

"The news story didn't give any reason

for his suicide," Clare said, testing the young man. "Do you have any idea what was behind it?"

Dick looked down at the carpet. "Sure, I heard a few things," he said in a low voice.

Hester stuck her head in the doorway from the kitchen again. "Ask him how he is doing in the market?"

Dick cast an angry glance toward his fiancée. "Now you cut that out!" he told her.

Hester rolled her eyes. "You're just not a good loser!" she told him, and disappeared again to finish getting dinner.

Clare gave the pilot an inquiring glance. "Have you had some bad luck with your investments?"

"You bet I have," Dick said dejectedly. "All the time I was away there was a run on the market. This pal of mine didn't want to sell without an okay from me. When I got back this morning, I found out my stocks are worth just half what they were when I left. I've lost almost all my paper profits."

"I'm sorry," Clare said.

"I'm through with the market," Dick said disconsolately. "I can't watch it closely enough." He paused to sigh. "At least I got the car out of it."

"I'm glad," Clare said. But she was still curious to find out what he knew about the suicide. She reminded him, "Before Hester interrupted, you were going to tell me what you'd heard about Burt Crandall."

Dick's boyish face wore a pained expression as he looked up at her. "You've got to promise me you won't say a word to anyone."

"Of course."

The young pilot swallowed hard. "There's been organized smuggling going on, and they've been using Trans-Continental flights from Europe," he said. "It's been happening for a long time. Mostly jewels. Some dope as well. The gossip is that Crandall was one of the ring."

Clare stared at him. "Do you believe it?"

Dick shrugged unhappily. "He must have had some strong motive for doing a thing like that."

Hester appeared in the doorway again. This time she directed her words to Clare. "Would you like to help me set the table, honey?" she asked.

"Sure," Clare said. She apologized by adding, "I should have helped you before, but I've been talking to Dick about the suicide."

"I know," Hester said in a dreary tone. "Isn't it awful!"

Clare was conscious of an atmosphere of

174

depression in the small apartment. She couldn't decide whether to blame the weather or Dick's losses in the stock market. But the other two were in a blue mood all during dinner and afterward. Hester said little while Clare helped her wash up the dishes. When they rejoined Dick in the living room, he was standing forlornly before the window, staring out at the rain.

Hester shot her boy friend a guilty glance. "You better tell her," she said.

Dick's pleasant face took on a crimson shade. "But it's just gossip," he protested. "Why bother her?"

"What are you two talking about?" Clare demanded.

"You tell her or I will," Hester warned Dick.

"Well?" Clare fixed her eyes on the uncomfortable young man.

He spread his hands in despair. "Hester is making a lot of fuss over nothing much. I told her something I heard, and she takes it as fact, which it probably isn't."

"Go on," Clare said, not daring to guess what might be about to be revealed. Had they found out she was working with Arnold Benson and the Federal men?

"It's about this smuggling," Dick said unhappily.

"Yes," Clare urged him on.

"Well," he said, "they've had their eyes on a few of the staff people. One of them was Burt Crandall. And the talk is there is someone else in the main office they think knows all about the racket."

"Who?"

Dick hesitated. Then in a low voice he said, "Harry."

Whatever she'd expected to hear, it hadn't been that. She gave a small gasp. "Harry! You must be joking."

"No!" he shook his head. "I'm serious. They say he's been making a lot of trips to London for the company and working on the shipments of the stolen gems at the same time."

"But that's ridiculous?" Clare exclaimed. She turned to Hester, "Don't you agree?"

"I only know what Dick told me," Hester said.

"But Harry just isn't the type!" Clare argued.

"That's what I say," the young pilot was quick to agree. "And I warned you this is pilot room gossip. There's no proof at all."

Clare didn't know what more to say. It was too utterly ridiculous. The tables had been turned with a vengeance. All along she had been suspecting Dick of getting his sudden wealth from the profits of smuggling and it turned out that it was Harry who might be guilty. It seemed too utterly fantastic.

Hester rose from the chair and came over to her. "Maybe I was wrong to make Dick tell you. But I thought you should hear it."

"I don't believe it," she said, still shocked.

The redheaded girl patted her arm. "I know how you feel. Of all your boy friends, I've always favored Harry. I think the rumor must be wrong."

"Sure. It's just a lot of talk because Harry has been making those trips overseas," Dick said. "I wouldn't give it two thoughts if I were you."

Clare gave him an unhappy look. "Let me know if you hear anything more," she said in a dull voice.

"You bet," the young pilot said.

"I have a headache," Clare told them. "Please excuse me!" And she hurried off to her own room. When she had closed the door after her, she threw herself on the bed and tried to think it all out. She'd felt on the brink of crying, but strangely no tears came.

Why would a rising young executive like Harry risk being involved in such a thing? What would his motive be, aside from the money to be gained, which wouldn't count in the long run? Was it an urge to live dangerously that had led him into this criminal activity? He had always been an impatient, restless type.

Those questions plagued her long into the night. And she determined to get in touch with Munson, the Federal man, in the morning and try and find out from him if there was any truth in the rumor. The knowledge that she had someone to turn to gave her some small satisfaction.

Neither she nor Hester mentioned the subject at breakfast the following morning. But as soon as Clare reported to the V.I.P. lounge, she phoned the number Munson had given her. A strange male voice answered and informed her that Munson was out of town. It was a numbing blow, since she'd counted on some help from the Federal man.

When noon hour came she was eager to get away from the lounge. She took the escalator downstairs and reached the main waiting room at a moment when it was filled with a confused movement of people arriving and departing on various flights.

Then she spotted Harry some distance away. He was standing close to one of the gates where passengers were arriving from an overseas flight. She was about to push her way through the milling throng to reach him when something happened that made her stand stock-still.

Harry suddenly took a few steps toward the gate, and as the incoming passengers streamed through he singled out a short, stocky man, approached and greeted him genially. As the two shook hands Clare clearly recalled who the newcomer was. It was Fritz Manner, the European financial manipulator who the Federal man had warned her might be the power behind the smuggling gang.

Chapter Eleven

Clare watched as the two men talked for a moment and then strolled off together in the direction of the large bar and restaurant which catered to the air line passengers. As they vanished in the crowd, she turned away. This visual evidence that Harry was really mixed up with Fritz Manner had come with shattering swiftness.

She no longer really felt hungry, and so, instead of going into the cafeteria, she stopped by a snack bar that served drinks and sandwiches. She ordered a glass of milk and stood there to drink it. Then she wandered aimlessly through the vast waiting room until it was time to return to the lounge.

She wondered what Harry and the shady financier would be talking about in the downstairs dining room. And then, when she received the check list of the passengers for the afternoon flight to Los Angeles, she found Fritz Manner's name. It gave her a start. So the mystery man wasn't remaining in New York long.

If the smuggling gang had contacts on the West Coast, he was probably going there to see them. She waited for him to appear in the V.I.P. lounge to see if Harry would still be with him. But when the stout, swarthy man showed up, he was alone.

He had a hawk face, deeply lined, and in spite of his excellently tailored clothes he gave the appearance of a gangster. The financier nodded to her as he came through the glass doors of the lounge.

"Is the flight to L.A. leaving on time?" he asked in a harsh voice.

She nodded. "Yes. All flights are leaving as scheduled."

The hawk face showed a bored expression. "I've seen you before, haven't I?" Fritz Manner asked.

"You may have," she said. "I've been here some time."

"I want to make some phone calls," Manner said brusquely.

She pointed to a distant wall. "There are a number of phones over there. No charge except for long distance calls. Just wait until the operator comes on the line and give her your number."

The financier scowled as he stared at the

bank of open phones along a shelf with stools in front of each phone. "They're out in the open!"

"Yes."

"What privacy do they give you?" he demanded angrily. "I prefer a pay phone booth."

"They have them down in the main waiting room," she said. "These are a special service to our V.I.P customers."

The hawk face showed disgust. "Some service!" he snapped. "I'll make my calls from downstairs." And he turned and strode out of the lounge angrily.

She did not see him again. But when the time came for passengers to board the Los Angeles flight, she went out on the promenade and watched for him among those lining up at the ramp. After a moment she spotted his stocky figure and saw him climb the steps and enter the jet.

When late afternoon arrived and she'd still had no word from Munson, she decided she would try to see Arnold Benson.

The prim secretary put her through to the general manager of Trans-Continental.

"May I have a short interview with you, Mr. Benson?" she asked.

"When?" the austere executive wanted to know.

"As soon as possible. Now if you can arrange it. I've seen Fritz Manner."

"I see." Arnold Benson sounded more interested. "Come along then, Miss Andrews. I'll squeeze you in between appointments."

When she presented herself to his secretary, she was shown into the large private office without delay. Arnold Benson came forward to greet her. "Well," he said, "what is the latest, Miss Andrews?

She told him about Fritz Manner, ending with, "I saw him get aboard the jet. So he is well on his way to Los Angeles by now."

The bald Benson nodded. "I already knew that he had arrived on the London flight and most of the other facts you've told me. Still, that bit about his not wanting to use the phones in the V.I.P lounge is significant."

Bracing herself, she asked the question that was really bothering her. "Do you suspect Harry Travis of being mixed up in this trouble?"

His gaze was icy. "Why do you ask me that?"

"I've heard the rumor since that pilot committed suicide. The story going the rounds is that others on the staff are connected with the smuggling ring, and one of them is Harry Travis."

Arnold Benson said, "I expect to obtain information from you, Miss Andrews; not hand it out."

Clare was undaunted. "I'm beginning to think that is why you chose me to report to you: so that you could keep a close check on me. You felt I might know what Harry is doing, since I've been his friend so long."

The executive's bony face showed a derisive expression. "Make what you like out of it, Miss Andrews."

"Then I must be right!"

"Not necessarily."

"Can you tell me anything about Harry?" she asked. "How much evidence you have against him?"

Arnold Benson smiled coldly. "I can only tell you the company is sending him to London again on business."

She stared at him. "You mean you're baiting a trap for him."

"I didn't say that. He frequently visits the London office."

"But this time it will be different!"

The executive's eyes narrowed. "Let me give you one bit of advice, Miss Andrews. Say nothing about any of our talks to him. So far you have a clean record with the company. Keep it that way."

"I'll try to remember that," she said, stunned by Arnold Benson's attitude.

"I expect your loyalty, Nurse Andrews," was his final word before he showed her out of the office.

She found herself more upset than before. As soon as she left the airport she went straight home to the apartment. She stretched out on the bed in her room and tried to get all that had happened clear in her mind.

She was still on the bed when Hester came home. The redhead came into her room and sat on the edge of the bed. "You're going to make yourself ill, honey," her friend said. "All this worrying isn't doing any good."

Clare stared up at the other girl. "Why?" she asked. "Why would he get involved in such a thing?"

"You're not sure that he is."

"I'm almost certain," Clare said, turning her head on the pillow and gazing forlornly out the window. "I'm asking myself if I could be to blame in any way. I've been deliberately cold to Harry lately."

"Nonsense!" Hester said.

Clare gave her a quick glance. "But you've accused me of that very thing," she reminded her. "Could he have gone into the smuggling to make fast money and impress me?"

"That wouldn't be like Harry," the other girl said.

"They're sending him to London again," Clare told her. "I wonder if I'll hear from him before he leaves."

"You know you will," Hester told her with exaggerated assurance.

As it turned out, she did. His phone call came just after dinner that evening. He sounded very much his ordinary self with no hint of strain in his manner.

He said, "The weather prediction is good for tomorrow. How about driving to the beach and having dinner at some roadside restaurant?"

She tried to sound casual. "It might be fun," she agreed.

"Then it's settled," Harry said. "I'm leaving for London again on Monday, and I'd like to have a talk with you before I go."

"Aren't they overdoing it?" she asked. "I mean by sending you overseas so often."

He laughed. "Not really. I've been working on some cost accounting problems in our London office. I didn't get them done when I was there before. But this time I should finish everything."

"I see," she said.

"What time will I come by for you?" he asked.

"How about two-thirty?"

"I'll be there on the dot," he promised. "That will allow us a leisurely drive to the shore and some time to enjoy the beach. And we'll have dinner wherever you like."

She put down the phone with a feeling of deep sadness.

Although Sunday was a fine day, it was still on the cool side. So the roads were not too crowded. Harry had arrived right on time, and they drove in the direction of the nearest large beach. They arrived there within a half-hour and parked the car. Hand in hand, they strolled along the almost deserted vast stretch of sandy beach. The tide was out, and they walked close to the water's edge.

Harry, in dark slacks and corduroy jacket, gave her a smile. "You've been unusually quiet today," he observed.

She avoided his glance, staring out at the wide expanse of ocean. A sailboat with yellow sails and a few other pleasure craft dotted it at intervals. Vaguely she said, "Have I?"

"You know you have," he accused her. "Is it deliberate?"

"No."

"You sulk so much of the time lately," he said with a sigh. "I hoped today would be different."

She looked at him briefly. "It is different."

"I don't think so."

"How do you want me to act?"

He shrugged. "I'd prefer that you didn't retreat into yourself like some of these little shell creatures we see here on the beach."

"I'm thinking," she said.

"About what?"

"A lot of things," she said, staring at the firm, wet sand as they walked across it.

"I hope you're still not mooning over that actor," Harry complained.

"Let's leave Boyle out of this."

"Okay," he said with resignation. "So what else is bothering you?"

"You seem to be changing," she told him. "You're nothing like the boy I used to know."

He halted and gave her an incredulous look. "Well, I like that," he said. "Whatever gave you that idea?"

"It's true," she said. "You've become cold and absorbed in other interests. I can hardly communicate with you."

Harry laughed curtly. "That's a joke," he said. "You're the one who has changed."

It was her turn to show surprise. "Why do you say that?"

His pleasant face registered anger now. "Because you've been drifting in a world of your own ever since you've been dating that Boyle Heath."

"You're wrong!" she protested.

"Don't tell me!" he said, facing her. "And the worst part of it is that he doesn't deserve a girl like you. He'd do nothing but make you unhappy."

"How would you know?" she challenged him, as they carried on their hot debate on the deserted beach.

"For one thing, he's too old for you. And for another, he's failed in two previous marriages."

"Which proves nothing," Clare said. "You're so jealous you can see no good in him!"

"Sure I'm jealous!" Harry admitted angrily.

"And what makes you think you're so much better than him?" she demanded. "Aren't you just as likely to bring me unhappiness?"

"Not knowingly," Harry said. And in an awkward tormented fashion, he added, "It just happens that I love you."

"Do you? I wonder."

"You needn't," he said. "We had the future nicely planned until Boyle came along to turn your head."

She said, "If that future was still open to us, could you take advantage of it? Live an ordinary, normal life?" She was thinking of his involvement in the smuggling.

"Marry me, Clare, and I'll prove that we can be happy," he said with an earnest expression on his young face. He took her in his arms and kissed her.

She pushed him away. Glancing up the beach, she said, "People will see us!"

He laughed. "There's no one around. And even if there were, haven't I the right to kiss the girl who's going to be my wife?"

"I didn't promise anything," she warned him.

"I'll not leave you until you say yes," he told her.

She started walking back along the beach in the direction of the car. "I saw you talking to Fritz Manner at the airport yesterday," she said.

"Oh?" He sounded slightly uneasy.

Clare looked at him sharply. "How do you two come to be such good friends?"

"We're not."

"You went off with him to the restaurant?"

Harry smiled at her. "That doesn't mean we're close friends. I've met him once or twice in London, in a business way."

"Air line business?"

"What else?" he asked in a convincing imitation of surprise.

"It doesn't seem likely he'd be transacting business with you," she said. "You're in the accounting division, not sales."

"I told you I was helping line up the costs of a construction job for the company in London," he said. "Fritz Manner is head of one of the outfits bidding for the project."

It was an acceptable alibi. She couldn't help but admire his skill in devising it so quickly. But she still wasn't convinced by it. She said, "Of course you know he has a shady reputation."

Harry took this calmly enough. "Most men of his type have."

She saw she was going to get nowhere with him unless she came out with her suspicions more directly. They had reached the car now. She turned to him before getting in it and asked, "What about the smuggling you told me about?"

He frowned. "I haven't heard anything lately."

"Now you're deliberately lying," she accused him. "You know that pilot, Burt

Crandall, committed suicide over it. And there are others involved."

"How do you know Crandall killed himself because of the smuggling?" he asked. "There was no tie-in with the smuggling in the newspaper accounts."

"It's being whispered all around the airport," she said. "Don't tell me you're the only one who didn't hear about it."

He was silent a moment. "I heard," he said at last. "I didn't mention it because I think there's been too much talk about it."

Her eyes met his. "Do you know more about it than the rest of us?"

"How could I?" he asked with such innocence that she realized she could hope for no confession of guilt from him.

She ended with a last word of warning. "I think you'd better be wary," she said, "especially when you're in London."

He opened the car door for her without giving any sign that her warning had meant anything to him. She waited for him to take his place behind the wheel, feeling that she'd failed. There was no hope of reaching him. So she said nothing as he backed the car up and headed it onto the main highway again.

They stopped for dinner at a good restaurant on the road leading into the city. In spite of her depression, the salt air of the beach had given her an appetite. Over an excellent meal, the cold reserve between them gave way a little.

Harry told her, "When I come back, we'll give ourselves time and straighten out all these misunderstandings."

She studied him across the table. "You think so?" she asked quietly.

So their day ended without the showdown she knew was inevitable.

Hester and Dick were still out somewhere when she let herself into the apartment. She was glad to be alone in her unhappy mood. Swiftly changing into her night things, she took a mild sedative and went to bed.

Monday proved to be a busy day. And Clare was thankful. It gave her a chance to submerge her personal unhappiness in the hectic activity of the V.I.P. lounge. Isobel also had news for her.

The blonde girl took the first opportunity they had to talk for a few minutes to tell her, "I'm being assigned to flight duty in two weeks."

"You've already applied for the transfer?"

Isobel nodded. "Yes. I have a chance to rent my apartment furnished. I think the sooner I make a break with the past the better."

"I agree." Clare smiled. "And I wish you luck. It means I'll have to break a new girl in here."

"I'm certain you'll find someone who wants this kind of job," Isobel said. "It's not that difficult."

"I needn't hope she'll be as congenial as you," Clare replied.

When she received the check list for the London flight she saw that Harry's name was on it. So there was no question that he was going overseas. She was certain Arnold Benson had devised some elaborate scheme to trick him into revealing his role in the smuggling. There was also another familiar name on the list, that of Gloria Faith.

Clare frowned as she studied the list. The Federal man had said that the star was still under suspicion. Did it mean something?

Her speculations were ended by passengers arriving for the overseas flight, climaxed by the appearance of Gloria Faith herself. She was still looking haggard, but as far as Clare could tell the star was cold sober. A big, bronzed man with a coarsely handsome face was at her side, and Clare guessed this must be her ex-husband and personal manager, Ben.

Gloria left the man to come over to Clare and embrace her. Having delivered a kiss on her cheek, the star told her smilingly, "I've been on my good behavior since our night in Chicago."

Clare asked, "Are you giving a concert in London?"

"And Glasgow and Birmingham and a dozen other cities," the former film star told her. She gave a glance in the direction of her companion, who was standing a distance away with a surly expression. And then in a low voice she confided, "I'd introduce you to Ben, but he honestly isn't worth the effort."

Clare talked with the star a few minutes more and then had to attend to a child that had developed a bad nose bleed. By the time she'd taken care of the youngster the loudspeakers were announcing boarding instructions for the flight.

All the other passengers had left when Harry came rushing into the lounge. He was breathless as he came over to her. "Got tied up," he said, "But I had to say goodbye."

"Good luck," she said quietly, thinking he would need it.

"We'll get together the minute I'm back," he told her again. And he bent down to give her a brief kiss. A smile brightened his youthful face. "It's going to be all right," he promised.

As she watched him go, she wanted to cry out a warning. But she didn't. And then it was too late.

Chapter Twelve

Two days after Harry left for London, the Federal man came to see Clare. She took him into her office and braced herself for whatever bad news he might have for her.

Munson's lined, square face was set in a stern expression. "Your friend is being closely watched in London," he told her.

"Oh?" she said lightly.

"You know who I mean," he went on. "Travis is almost certain to make a false step this time. Did he say anything to you before he left?"

"Nothing but goodbye."

The Federal man showed annoyance. "I'm not interested in jokes, Miss Andrews."

"I'm simply telling you the truth."

"I'm wondering how you two could be such close friends and you not find out anything about this gem business."

"There could be a simple explanation," she suggested. "Harry may not be guilty."

"We think he is."

"You were suspicious of René Le Blanc," she reminded him.

"That was different," the Federal man told her. "Your boy friend knows too many of the wrong people. And he's made trips at the exact times shipments of stolen jewels have been landed over here."

"So must a lot of other people," she pointed out. "The planes carry a good many."

"But most of them are not repeaters," Munson said. "I don't blame you for being loyal to Travis. But you better prepare yourself for trouble. He's likely to be arrested as soon as he sets foot back here."

So that was that! She worried through the week. And then on Monday she received a cablegram from Boyle Heath. The message was terse: "Flying back to arrive Tuesday at noon. Love, Boyle."

Since the trouble involving Harry, she'd given little thought to the handsome actor. This came to her as a shock. She hadn't actually wondered when he would return or worried about how he was making out. It made her question whether it had been love or sympathy she'd felt for the temperamental, aging star. Still, it would be good to see him again.

When she returned home that night, she told Hester that Boyle was returning the next day. She offered her friend a perplexed smile. "What makes me wonder is that I haven't really missed him."

Hester was definite. "You're not in love with Boyle."

"I thought I was."

"And all you've been doing is worrying about Harry Travis. If you care for anyone, it's Harry," the redhead said.

Clare sighed.

"Maybe it will still turn out all right," Hester said optimistically. "Dick doesn't think he's guilty."

"Dick is his friend."

"And that means he knows him well enough to judge," Hester said. "And so do we. I don't think he'd be mixed up with a lot of crooks either."

"I did see him talking to that Fritz Manner."

"He told you he'd met him through air line business."

"And I have no way of checking his story," Clare pointed out. Then with a sigh, she added, "I guess we'll find out the truth soon enough. Munson says he'll face arrest as soon as he returns from London."

"That Federal man may only have been trying to frighten you into telling him anything you know," Hester said.

"I wish it was settled," Clare worried, "no matter how it turns out."

The following morning when Clare received her list of passengers coming in on the noon flight from London, she was surprised to see that Harry Travis was also going to be on that plane. He and Boyle would be returning to New York on the same flight. And Gloria Faith's name was another she recognized. It now seemed likely developments were liable to take place rapidly in the resolution of the gem smuggling racket.

Around eleven o'clock it began to rain, and a light fog moved in on the airport. The dismal weather matched Clare's own mood. She could not develop any enthusiasm for the arrival of the jet bringing Harry back, since he would in all likelihood be met by Munson and other Federal men.

She was carefully instructing an elderly woman on how to take the air sickness tablets she had given her when a troubled-looking Isobel came over and asked to speak with her privately. Clare quickly wound up her lecture to the elderly passenger and joined her assistant.

"What's the matter?" she asked. "You look ill?"

"I've had bad word about the noon flight from London," the blonde girl said.

"They're just off the coast, and they have a fire aboard."

"A fire?"

Isobel nodded. "An electrical fire. It's knocked out all the lights and interfered with its wireless."

"Harry is on that plane," Clare said, feeling ill, "and Boyle Heath, not to mention Gloria Faith and a lot of others."

"There are a hundred and sixty-two passengers aboard her," Isobel said.

Clare gave her an agonized glance. "How bad is the fire?"

"I don't know," Isobel said. "I've told you all I've been able to find out. The word is spreading all around the airport. They're sending out an emergency ground crew to prepare for a crash landing."

Clare listened numbly. It had been a long time since there'd been a major crash at Kennedy. And now it seemed their good luck had run out; a disaster was at this moment in the making. It would be doubtful if the pilot of the Boeing 707-320 would manage to get the big jet to the airport. Fire could race through a plane with frightening swiftness once it got under way. Depending on how bad the blaze was, the huge plane could plunge into the Atlantic at any moment.

Clare looked around and saw that the passengers in the lounge had split up into small groups. The clusters of four and six people were tense faced and talking seriously. It took no mind reader to guess that the rumors about the jet in distress were spreading wildly.

Clare said, "I've got to find out more about what's happening."

Isobel sighed. "It will be hard to get exact information."

Clare gave her a meaningful glance. "They'll know at the control tower."

"Yes. But there's no use phoning. The lines will be blocked."

Clare had made a decision. "You look after things. I'm going to go over there and get the news." She started for the door.

Isobel followed her. "Do you think you should?"

Clare didn't slacken her steps. "I must," was her firm reply.

She took the escalator and then hurried across the waiting room to the nearest exit. Unmindful of the rain and the fact that she'd neglected to bring her raincoat, she stood waiting for one of the Trans-Continental service jeeps to pass so she could hitch a ride to the control tower.

Of course none was in sight. She turned

up the collar of her uniform and realized she was trembling. As she stood there waiting impatiently, she pictured what might be taking place aboard the stricken jet. After the first acrid odor of smoke seeped through the plane, there would be a general alarm. If the lights had failed, there would be hysteria among some of the passengers as the stewardesses went among them with flashlights in an attempt to keep order. The captain would show himself and explain what had happened and the emergency precautions. Life belts would be groped for in the darkness and fastened on with fingers shaking with fear. The stewardesses would check those they had time to, and a shocking number of life belts would be found to be strapped on improperly. The captain would call out the locations of the safety exits and how to get through them — first one foot, then head and shoulders, followed by the other foot. Red flames would shoot past the windows; there would be horrifying rattles from the engines along with screeching sounds; and increasing by the minute heavy, choking smoke!

She almost screamed out at her own imagined picture of the panic aboard the blazing jet. And somewhere in the midst of it all were Harry Travis and Boyle Heath.

A jeep with the familiar Trans-Continental crest came by, and she shouted and stepped out almost directly in front of it. The driver jammed on his brakes and came to a screeching stop on the wet asphalt.

Sticking his head out of the cab, he said angrily, "You've got your nerve, lady!"

She was already opening the other door and getting in beside him. "Take me to the control tower," she ordered.

He stared at her, his fat face a comic picture of surprise. "Who are you orderin' around?" he wanted to know. "I've got my work to do."

"Please!" she begged. "Don't waste any time. Take me to the control tower. It's urgent!"

"Yeah?" He hesitated, still skeptical.

"If you don't do as I say, I'll report you to Mr. Benson, our general manager," she said, frantic to persuade him to do as she asked.

The driver of the jeep eyed her dubiously. "What's this about you having to get to the control tower?"

She knew she had to come up with something plausible. "The phone is blocked and I have an important message for them. It's about that jet that is on fire."

"No kidding." The driver sounded impressed at last. "I'll have you there in a jiffy, lady," he promised as the jeep shot forward.

He was almost as good as his word. Within a spectacularly short space of time, he let her out at the control tower. She raced inside and took the elevator to the upper floor. Her uniform and hair were drenched, and rain rippled down her cheeks. When she stepped from the elevator she saw a strange tableau in the big room. A circle of people were gathered around two of the air controllers who she guessed were in contact with the blazing jet.

No one paid the scantest attention to her as she edged forward to join the circle. There was a confused babble, and she could make nothing out of it. Then she suddenly spotted her friend, Joe, and elbowed her way to him. The thin man looked down with a startled expression as she tugged at his arm.

"Have they crashed?" she asked tensely.

"No," he said. "But the blaze has fouled up their wireless. We've lost communication with them."

"How close are they?"

"Should be coming in for a landing soon," Joe said. He shrugged. "In this weather and without proper operational facilities, it's a question whether they'll make it."

"You think they'll crash on the landing strip?"

"Looks mighty like it," Joe said. "They're out there waiting for them now."

Clare was completely frustrated. After her rush to get to the control tower, she'd arrived too late. She dug her fingers into Joe's arm. "Take me out there!"

He turned to give her his full attention. "Say, you're in a bad state!"

"Harry Travis is on that plane," she said frantically. "I want to be there when it lands. They may need nurses. Please take me!"

Joe looked at her uncertainly. After a moment's deliberation, he said, "All right. Come on."

The rain was coming down harder than before. Joe drove as close as he could to the area where the jet was expected to attempt a landing. A huge section was roped off, and a coating of foam had been spread over the airstrip as a fire precaution. As she and Joe got out of his car and walked toward the roped area, she was conscious of the quiet that had come over part of the huge airport. There was no sound. Ambulances, doctors, firemen, police reporters and members of the Trans-Continental staff waited tensely. With their uniforms to identify them, Joe and Clare had no difficulty moving up to the spot where the ambulances were parked.

Then, from high above the clouds, came the ominous sound of the crippled jet approaching. Clare strained to catch some sign of it through the haze of fog and rain. All at once the roar of it was terrifyingly near, and its bulk showed through the mist as it bore down on the landing strip with its floor of chemical foam. On it came. Swiftly and surely its wheels touched the ground, and it held its course. It never swerved, but as it lost speed it tilted slightly on its nose. But there was no fire, no explosion. The crowd shouted with relief as the various services rushed forward to the jet.

Smoke was still showing from it, and it soon became clear that what had seemed to the spectators like an easy landing had been anything but that. In the impact of the jolting halt, a number of the passengers had suffered at least minor injuries. The majority of them were victims of smoke inhalation. Clare made herself known to the doctor in charge and was at once put to work assisting the less severely injured passengers into ambulances. It was routine that all should have hospitalization and a check.

She had just returned from seeing an elderly man to one of the ambulances when they carried Harry off the plane on a stretcher. His face was pale, and he was unconscious. A swift query from the intern walking beside the stretcher informed her he'd suffered a concussion. Praying that he might not be too badly hurt, she returned to help the other passengers. And it was then that Boyle Heath came toward her, leaning on one of the firemen for support. His face was bleeding from a cut on his left cheek, his hair was disheveled, and he was limping badly. She ran to meet him.

"Boyle, are you all right?" she asked.

He managed a wan smile. "Sure. Nothing wrong that a couple of martinis can't fix. I thought we were finished up there."

"I know," she said. "So did I. Harry was just brought off the plane. He seems to be badly hurt. I think his ambulance has already gone."

"Too bad," Boyle said. "I was one of the lucky ones. I'll just get me a taxi and head into town."

One of the doctors had joined them. Recognizing the television star, he said, "Take Mr. Heath to the first ambulance."

Boyle let go of the fireman and stood with wobbly dignity as he told the doctor, "I don't need to go to a hospital. I'm in good shape."

"You don't look it," the medical man said brusquely. "Please don't delay us with arguments. There are still people on the plane to be taken care of."

The fireman made a move to support the actor again, but Boyle Heath uttered an angry oath and pushed him away. Then he made a pathetic effort to hobble to the sidelines where the reporters' cars were parked. Two or three of them shouted encouragement to him as they took his picture from various angles.

Clare hurried after him, calling, "Wait, Boyle! The doctor is right!"

The actor turned to reply but never did speak. Instead, he collapsed in a heap on the wet asphalt. Clare shouted for help, and two of the stretcher bearers went over and got him. Within a matter of minutes he was being placed in an ambulance.

The last of the plane's passengers were being removed now. And one of them was Gloria Faith. She was also a stretcher case, but conscious. When Clare approached her, the actress gave her a look of recognition.

"My friend from the air line," she murmured.

"We'll have you in a hospital in just a little while," Clare promised her.

"I'm really no emergency case," the former film star protested. "I've only a broken leg."

"That's bad enough," Clare said. "Are you comfortable?"

The woman on the stretcher said, "Yes. The doctor gave me something. It helped a great deal."

"The worst is over," Clare said.

"The funny thing is Ben refused to take this flight," the star went on. "He's coming over tomorrow. He seems to have a nose for failures." And she smiled bitterly.

Gloria Faith was moved into an ambulance, and there were only a half-dozen after that. When the last of the crew and passengers were safely on their way, Clare let Joe drive her back to the Trans-Continental terminal building.

The big man gave her a side glance as he drove through the rain. "That's something we'll always remember."

"But it turned out well," she said. "Not a single person was killed."

"Don't be too sure," Joe warned her. "I heard one of the doctors say there were two or three in critical condition."

Clare at once pictured the wan, motionless Harry as she'd seen him on the stretcher, and her throat tightened with fear for him. She said, "I must find out what hospital they've taken them to."

"As far as I could tell by their talk, they were dividing them between two hospitals," Joe said.

And he proved to be right. It took her only a short time to find out that Harry was a patient at Manhattan General. She stopped at the lounge long enough to let Isobel know she'd be gone for the rest of the day and then took a taxi to the hospital.

A period of waiting was required before she was able to talk to a doctor about Harry. The hospital staff had been taxed by the sudden influx of patients, even though most of them were not in too serious a condition. She was finally able to have a few minutes with the doctor who was attending Harry.

He was an elderly man and sympathetic. "Your friend received a nasty head injury," he said. "But I do not consider his condition critical."

"Has he recovered consciousness?" Clare wanted to know.

"Not yet," the doctor said. "He may remain in a coma for an indefinite time."

"I see," she said quietly.

The doctor patted her arm. "Don't be so downcast," he told her. "My guess is that he'll be over it by this time tomorrow. As soon as he emerges from the coma, his recovery will be swift."

She gave the old man a grateful glance. "Thank you, doctor."

It wasn't until she received this welcome assurance that she began to wonder what had happened to Boyle Heath. An inquiry at the desk downstairs made it clear he was not at the hospital. She felt she could do no less than take a taxi to the other hospital where the injured from the jet had been sent. It was only a few blocks away, and the taxi trip took only a short time.

She entered the vast lobby of the second hospital and made her way to the desk to find out where Boyle Heath's room was located. So intent was she on her mission that she didn't notice Munson standing there.

The Federal man caught her attention by speaking to her. "Looking for somebody, Miss Andrews?"

She halted and gave him a startled look. "You."

He nodded. "That's right. I get around."

"I've come to see Boyle Heath," she said.

The Federal man gave her an odd glance. Taking her by the arm, he moved her a short distance from the desk to a spot where they were able to talk with some privacy. He said,

"I'm afraid you won't be able to see him, Miss Andrews."

"Why not?" she asked, sensing that something was terribly wrong.

His square face was grave. "Boyle Heath is dead."

"Oh, no," she protested.

"That's the story."

"What happened? He seemed well enough. He didn't want to come to the hospital. He tried to walk away before he collapsed."

"He died out there when he fell," the Federal man said. "That's as near as the doctors can figure it. He was dead in the ambulance. They say he must have had a heart condition, and the shock was too much for him."

"I can't believe it!" she said, stunned by the news.

"There are some other things about him that are hard to believe," Munson said grimly. "Did you know he had an artificial leg, that his left leg had been amputated above the knee?"

"No. I knew he limped. But he said he'd hurt his leg in Switzerland."

The Federal man sighed. "He probably was operated on in Switzerland. At any rate, he'd kept it a secret all these years. There was nothing on his passport to indicate he was an amputee."

"Poor Boyle!" she said sadly. "He was probably afraid it would hurt his popularity as a leading man if the public knew he had only one leg."

"Could be," Munson agreed. "But anyway, that's why he tried to keep out of the hospital. He knew he'd be exposed. And he especially didn't want that to happen today." He paused. "Not when he had thirty thousand dollars in stolen jewels hidden in the leg."

Clare stared at the Federal man. "What are you saying?"

"I'm saying that Boyle Heath was the key man in the gem smuggling. He used that fake leg to transport the stuff. He could have gone on for years without us finding out."

She found it difficult to grasp. "Boyle was mixed up in the smuggling."

Munson nodded. "We've known that since yesterday. Our men picked up Fritz Manner trying to dispose of some of the loot in Los Angeles. He talked in the hope of easing his own sentence. He provided the backing for their operations, Burt Crandall was their man on the Trans-Continental staff, and Boyle was the messenger."

"That's all there were?"

"That's all."

Clare studied him anxiously. "Then Harry wasn't one of them?"

"No. In spite of the fact he knew Manner, he had nothing to do with the smuggling. We think Manner was probably trying to win his friendship in the hope of using him later. He's a pretty slick customer."

She was still astounded from the effect of one shock coming upon another. She shook her head. "I don't think I really believe any of it yet."

The Federal man smiled. "I can understand that. But you will accept it gradually. It's been interesting working with you, Miss Andrews. I imagine this is goodbye. I can't picture us meeting again."

"I hope not," Clare said, attempting a smile in return. "Nothing personal, of course."

"I understand," the Federal man said. "And good luck to you and your young man."

At the moment Clare was none too certain that his wishes would come true. She was so badly shaken by her experiences that she phoned the air line the following morning and left a message that she would require another day to recuperate. Then she called the hospital; the report on Harry was that his condition had not changed.

Hester left for work after a final word of encouragement. "He'll get better, honey. He just has to!"

Clare still worried. In the early afternoon she made another visit to the hospital. When she reached the floor on which Harry's room was located, she ran into the elderly doctor in charge of his case. He was taking the elevator as she was leaving it.

He smiled at her. "I told you," he said. "He's conscious. You can see him. But stay only a few minutes." The elevator doors shut the doctor off from her.

Elated, she rushed down the corridor to Harry's room. The door was slightly ajar, and she entered on tiptoe. Reaching the bedside, she saw that his eyes were open. Seeing her, he smiled.

"A rough trip," he said weakly.

"But you made it safely," she said. "That's all that counts."

"Sure," he said, staring at her with fond eyes. "About those differences, I'm too weak to settle them now. Doesn't matter anyway. We'll have it all your way."

"Our way," she corrected him. "Marriage is the best kind of partnership. And I wouldn't dream of beginning ours by breaking the rules." And she bent down to seal the bargain with a kiss.